THE LAST KNIGHT

THE CURSED KINGDOM

HILDIE McQUEEN

USA TODAY BESTSELLING AUTHOR

OLIVERHEBERBOOKS

Cover art by Dar Albert, Wicked Smart Designs

Published by Oliver-Heber Books

0 9 8 7 6 5 4 3 2 1

Chapter One

Gunther Janssen made his way toward the balcony that overlooked the castle's courtyard, his tall form draped in thick velvet-like fabric that floated from his wide shoulders to his ankles.

Dark as the surroundings and oppressive as the air in the gloomy corridor, the midnight-black floor length cloak swayed around his body, the hem of it barely brushing the cold stone floor.

An enormous army had gathered, correction, *his* enormous army was assembled. Hundreds of soulless creatures and humans loyal to the darkness stood in wait, anticipating his directives. The air sizzled with expectation, everyone wanting to know where he would take the Dark Realm, the kingdom over which he was now ruler.

It was ironic that the realm that had claimed his existence for centuries and had sapped his soul was now his to rule while, at the same time, a prison from which he could not escape.

The feeble light flickering from the evenly spaced sconces along the walls cast long shadows across his path. There was no brightness in the Dark Realm, even in the middle of the day, it was rare that the suns' rays managed to permeate the thickness of the mists surrounding the realm.

In Gunther's opinion, the darkness was an apt punishment for the offences he'd committed. So many wrongs that even asking a higher power for forgiveness, which he'd done time and again, would never redeem him. In his core, there were times when Gunther understood the harsh sentence he'd lived through, of being held prisoner for hundreds of years.

Bitterness filled the back of his throat as the sky came into view. He was the supreme law of the realm, a sort of king. Albeit his kingdom was one filled with the screams of those held captive, blood running freely across stone floors, and an army of soulless creatures that never hesitated to maim or kill. There was no remorse in the Dark Realm, no pity and certainly no redemption.

One thing Gunther was sure of was that one misstep in his new role would lead to being overthrown, killed by the many who deemed him unworthy. Every time he thought about it, he wasn't sure if that was a good thing or a bad thing. On one hand, to be killed would mean finally being free. However, deep in his being, Gunther felt that there was a reason he'd lived so long and if he were to be honest, he wasn't ready to die, not yet.

For the first time in his life, he'd found something to look forward to. Did he dare to admit that a flicker of hope had birthed within his tattered soul? Of course, to expect redemption, forgiveness or even to be worthy of the miniscule amount of anticipation, he felt was ludicrous.

It was nonsensical how many times, he pictured a particular woman, repeated in his mind the scant minutes spent in the presence of the one person who'd called to the very essence of who he was. He wasn't a fool; nothing would ever come of it. After all, his fate was sealed, bound and locked. And yet, there was no harm in just a bit of light in his dark existence.

Two guards fell in line behind him as he stepped out onto the wide balcony that had always been used to address the Dark Army. At the hush of voices and the sight of hundreds of eyes lifting to him a surge of energy swelled within. Every pore of his body hummed as the magic coursed through Gunther's veins, sending pulses of intoxicating elixir to each of his senses. His vision was becoming so keen, he could see every expression and notice each movement in the forest beyond. Scents assaulted him, both good and bad, and he inhaled deeply enjoying the wonder of it. A noise caught his attention on the ground below. There in the far corner of the courtyard, a mouse urged another along, scampering across an open space to find a perfect place to hide, their soft squeaks as audible as if he was mere inches from them.

Relishing the moment, Gunther took a few minutes to hear, see and smell the surroundings before finally addressing the crowd below.

"As your leader, you are beholden to me now. I am to be called Gunther, nothing more. I do not require titles such as lord or master."

There were grunts of agreement from the creatures

below, whether they liked him or not, Gunther didn't care. What he would not tolerate would be any dissidents. "If any of you do not wish to serve me, then move to the north side of the courtyard."

There were exchanges of looks and murmurs until finally a group of about ten moved to stand together on the northern portion of the courtyard.

The group was made up of mostly humans, perhaps those captured by Meliot, his predecessor, and kept against their will. Despite gaining the dead wizard's powers, Gunther had not gained insight as to why some of the many who lived in the Dark Realm were held or lived there voluntarily.

"Who are you?" he called down, pinning one of the men who'd moved from the main group with his gaze.

The man held his chin high, his eyes lifted, meeting Gunther's directly. "We were all brought here against our will, part of a curse. We wish to be returned to our homes."

Gunther slid a glance to one of the guards, who peered down at the group of ten men with undisguised glee. Others who'd not moved did the same, waiting for the group who'd dissented to be punished.

There was little choice, an example had to be made.

Gunther held out his right hand, palm facing the group. None of the men flinched, instead they stood tall, prepared to face their fate. If he was down there, had been given the choice, he would have chosen death over remaining captive.

A flash of light erupted from his palm, engulfed the group of ten and within seconds, they were gone, only smoke remaining where they'd stood.

The soulless army cheered, holding up either fists or

whatever weapons they carried as they grunted, called out in their native tongues and stomped their boots into the ground.

Gunther lifted both hands, silencing the crowd. "Your commanders will inform each unit about what is expected in the following days."

With that he turned on his heel. One of the guards stepped into his path. "Gunther, you are expected to choose one of the warriors and reward him."

"For?"

"Exemplary action."

"I am the new leader and will decide which practices will continue." He met the man's gaze straight on. "Never step into my path again."

The guard gave a subtle nod, face expressionless, and moved aside.

At the previous ruler's death, there were many vying to take over one day. When Gunther lived among the warriors, he'd heard rumors of a plan to kill the wizard, because whomever committed the act would gain Meliot's powers. What no one had expected was for Gunther, one of the enslaved humans to be present in the room when Meliot was killed by a man destined to disappear from the realm.

He'd not asked for it and if given the choice would have not taken it. The only saving grace was that perhaps he could wrong some rights.

Upon returning to the throne room, he removed his cape and threw it over a chair, then he went to a bank of windows and peered out into the dim sky. A soft curve bending the corners of his lips, he let out a long breath.

The men he'd made disappear were returned to where they'd come from with a long road ahead, some having been held captive for a decade or more. But at last, they were free, and it felt good.

Oh, but the darkness, the magic that coursed through him was intoxicating, it was taking over there was no denying it. Soon he would become as cruel and unjust as his predecessor.

CHAPTER TWO

"Namaste," Aubrey Macguire bent at the waist and so did her students. Conversations about what the rest of the day held began as the ten ladies who'd attended rolled up their mats, expertly tying them into straps that could be slung over their shoulders.

One woman, a pretty redhead, waved goodbye to Aubrey before walking to where she'd left her bicycle.

The village where Aubrey lived was small enough that people who lived there could walk or bicycle everywhere. Except for those, like her, who lived on the outskirts.

Ashcraig Hall, the large estate that Aubrey called home, was about ten miles from the village, just far enough that she drove her 1992 red MG, a car she'd finally convinced her father to give to her.

Thankfully the weather was pleasant, sunny with a cool wind, so she could run errands without worry of rain. After storing her mat and Bluetooth speaker in the MG, Aubrey made her way to the first task on her list, the market. The cooler temperature and soft music filled the space as she pulled the door open and entered. There were only a few things on her list, but she meandered, perusing the shelves, in case something caught her interest. When she eased the shopping basket onto the counter, emptying the contents one by one, a bored looking clerk gave a lukewarm smile, taking to the task with slow movements as Aubrey placed each item into her tote.

Glancing at her watch, Aubrey hurried to meet her friend. Zina waved her over with more enthusiasm than their usual coffee date called for. She sat outside the village café, which was perfect since Aubrey had planned to ask that they enjoy the sunny weather.

"I can't wait to share something with you!" Zina shrieked.

"Can we get coffee first?" Aubrey asked with a wide grin, her gaze sweeping over her friend. "I would ask how you are, but it seems you're great."

"Coffee, yes, great idea." Zina hurried inside and Aubrey followed. Her friend went to the counter and leaned forward to study the menu. "We'll take two lattes and two croissants." She smiled at Aubrey. "My treat please."

Aubrey narrowed her eyes. "Whatever your announcement is, you're making me nervous. You only offer to pay on my birthday."

They returned to the same table.

Zina met Aubrey's gaze with intensity. "Guess what?"

"I have no idea."

Zina bit her bottom lip, her lips curving into a grin. "Guess something."

A long breath escaped. "All right, you got a promotion."

"Oh," Zina frowned. "I did. Totally forgot to tell you, I got a raise, but it was tiny. I'm sure I got the so-called promotion to quiet me since I found out Emma got a raise." Zina worked at a solicitor's office and had an ongoing feud with her coworker. She brightened again. "But that's not what my announcement is."

A young woman neared and placed the coffee and croissants on the table's surface. Aubrey thanked her while Zina didn't seem to notice.

"Jeffrey asked me to move in with him. He said we should start thinking about getting married." Zina spoke so fast, Aubrey wasn't sure she heard right.

"But you just started dating..." she began.

"No we haven't, girl, it's been almost a year," Zina exclaimed. "Besides, we see each other almost daily." They'd actually started dating closer to five months ago, but they had known each other much longer.

Aubrey's stomach did funny things. Her appetite disappeared. Zina had met Jeffrey through her and her ex-boyfriend, Marcus, who was Jeffrey's best friend. Just weeks after Zina and Jeffrey started dating, Marcus announced he wanted to see other people.

After dating for three years, the sudden breakup had taken a toll on Aubrey, sending her into a deep sadness that had lingered for months. Now Zina and Jeffrey were taking the next step in their relationship.

Since Aubrey's cousin Erin had recently married a wonderful man who doted on her and now Zina taking another step with Jeffrey, her closest friends were pairing up.

She was happy for them, but it would be trickier to do spontaneous things now.

"You will have to be my maid of honor, there is no question," Zina continued oblivious to Aubrey's silence. "Isn't it exciting!"

Just looking at Zina's face made Aubrey smile widely. She stood, rounded the table and hugged Zina. "I am super happy for you. I can't wait to help you plan the wedding. What about an engagement before we start picking colors and such?"

"Oh, it's coming," Zina proclaimed holding up her ringless hand. "I feel it in my bones." She gave Aubrey an endearing look. "You're next. Your aura is ripe for the picking."

"That's the coffee speaking," Aubrey replied, settling back down and sipping her latte. "When my day comes, I'm sure no one will be more surprised than me, the professional bridesmaid."

AN HOUR LATER, Aubrey pulled up the round drive that came to the front of her home, a stately estate called Ashcraig Hall, which she'd inherited, along with her cousin Erin. The mansion and surrounding acreage was much too big for them, but they'd grown up there and felt a kinship to the property. They could never sell it.

As she trudged up the steps to the front door, canvas tote in hand, a huge orange cat stood and stretched by the front door with an expression of superiority. Only Oscar, a former stray, with one cloudy eye, probably from an encounter with another cat, and a jagged ear could accomplish a stance of regal indignance and get away with it.

"Hello Oscar, I apologize for my tardiness," Aubrey said to the cat. "I bought you some sardines."

Together they walked into the house and straight to the kitchen. Aubrey made sure to fetch the sardines first, placed a couple onto a small dessert plate, and presented the meal to the cat.

Oscar was barely impressed, slowly eating the proffered treat.

It was almost three in the afternoon, and she had plans to cook a nice meal for her cousin, Erin, and Erin's new husband, Padriag Clarre, who were returning from their honeymoon that evening.

Soon the house would not be as empty since the couple would be living there while building a new home on land that belonged to Padriag.

Their story was a complicated one, a fairy tale of sorts. Aubrey still had a hard time believing that not only had Padriag been trapped in another realm, another reality, but that Erin had been instrumental in saving him.

Some days, she did her best to repress the things that she herself had gone through firsthand during the harrowing experience, however, current recurring incidents made it hard. Once her cousin and new husband settled, she needed to discuss what was happening to her with both of them.

IT WAS late afternoon when Aubrey headed to the kitchen to begin preparations for their dinner.

A swift breeze blew through the room and Aubrey froze, eyes wide, scanning the surroundings.

She more sensed than saw a figure appear in her periphery, whatever or whoever it was, was tall and broad shouldered, but when she tried to turn to see the figure, it faded.

"Find it. You must find it." The disembodied voice was many voices at once, some deep, some high. The words seemed to float in the air, repeating.

Aubrey closed her eyes and covered her ears and took deep breaths. "Stop it," she whispered.

"Who are you talking to?" Erin's voice made her jump.

"M-my addled brain," Aubrey hedged and studied the couple. Both of them radiated that unmistakable post-vacation glow, sun-kissed, relaxed, and practically humming with happiness. They looked like they'd spent days basking in paradise and sunshine, not a care in the world. Even Padriag, a natural redhead had somehow managed to pick up a warm, flattering hue that made him look almost golden.

Erin rushed to her and hugged her tightly. "It was so much fun."

Padriag stood back and smiled. "It was an enjoyable time, but it is good to be back."

Once the hugs and excited greetings were over, Aubrey waved them out of the kitchen with a mock-stern expression. "Go unpack and rest. I'll whip something up for dinner, and you can tell me all about your adventures."

Whether she'd unpacked or simply ditched their bags to hurry back, it wasn't long before Erin reappeared, a small velvet pouch in her hand and a sparkle in her eye. "I got you something," she said, and placed the bag in Aubrey's palm.

Inside was a delicate pair of porcelain earrings, hand-painted, floral, and utterly dainty. Aubrey went to the mirror on the wall next to the back entrance and held them up to her ears, the soft gleam catching the sunlight. "They're gorgeous," she whispered turning to her cousin. Her voice trembled slightly, and a shimmer of tears welled in her eyes. She swiped at them with the back of her hand and awkwardly held the earrings up in front of her face, as if admiring them could somehow mask the emotion that had blindsided her.

But growing up practically glued at the hip meant Erin could read her like a book. She crossed her arms slowly, one brow arching in that signature no-nonsense way. Her voice was gentle but firm. "Okay...what happened?"

Aubrey forced a smile, though she was sure it didn't quite reach her eyes. "Nothing," she said softly. "I'm just happy you're back. I missed you."

Without pressing further, she slipped the earrings back into their pouch and set them gently on the kitchen island.

Erin's gaze never wavered. "Wine?"

Aubrey nodded, grateful for something to do. "I'll pour." Aubrey's voice sounded high pitched to her own ears, and she cleared her throat. She poured two glasses.

"Zina and Jeffrey are moving in together, and she said he suggested they start planning a wedding. Isn't that great?" She held out a glass and Erin took it.

They went to the kitchen table next to a picture window overlooking a side garden. Roses in shades of yellow, red, and white, swayed in the gentle breeze, their beautiful blooms remaining regal. Needing the fresh air, Aubrey jumped up and opened a window, allowing the fragrance into the space.

"Stop stalling," Erin said and took a sip of the Pinot Noir. "Something is up, and now you're worrying me."

"This is going to sound very petty, which is why I am hesitant to share." Her eyes stung and she wanted to curse. Why was she so emotional?

Erin leaned forward, eyes wide with concern. "Aubrey?"

"Fine, I will tell you. But it really is very silly. I am hormonal, which is probably why I'm so weepy."

She let out a breath. "After Zina made the announcement about them moving in together and then asked me to be a bridesmaid, it made me angry, and probably jealous. I don't want to be her fucking bridesmaid. I don't want to ever be a bridesmaid again. Why does everyone automatically ask me to be in their wedding? It's almost like they pity me."

"I didn't ask you to be in my wedding," Erin whispered.

"That's because you didn't want a traditional wedding. Otherwise, I know you would have insisted on it." Aubrey looked up to the ceiling. "I am not making any sense am I?"

With a soft smile, Erin took Aubrey's hand. "I know exactly how you feel. And no, you're not being petty. It sucks to see everyone around you finding a partner. It was exactly how I felt when all my friends found partners, except I had you."

"I don't have you. Not anymore," Aubrey whispered. "Your husband should be your priority, and although I know you will always be there for me, it isn't the same. It never will be."

Silence fell over them, there was nothing to be said, because both knew that it was true. It didn't matter if they saw each other every day, Erin was a married woman now, the invisible yet very tangible line that should not be crossed was drawn.

Over the years they'd had all matter of conversations at that table. They'd discussed clothes, music, boys. Had laughed, cried and mourned in that room, with and without other members of the family. It seemed only right that this latest chapter, the beginning of a new way of life was discussed there.

"Don't suggest I start dating," Aubrey said holding up a hand. "Zina began suggesting single men Jeffrey knew after the bridesmaid comment." She rolled her eyes. "As if moving in with a guy makes her a relationship expert."

Erin laughed. "She has always claimed to be an expert on all matters of the heart. You know she means no harm."

"I know," Aubrey acquiesced. Glancing over to the kitchen counter, she spoke again. "I am going to make a yummy dinner for you both tonight. Go rest up."

AFTER ERIN LEFT THE KITCHEN, Aubrey went to her bedroom and retrieved her journal, with her journal in hand and a square wicker basket filled with pens and journalling ephemera, she returned to the kitchen table.

In truth, she had little to complain about. Hers was a blessed life. No financial worries. Thanks to her father's shrewd investments, there was a healthy trust fund for her. She was well physically and had the freedom to do work she adored. If anything was missing, it was undoubtedly her own choice, as she'd always turned down any matchmaking efforts. Not to mention, she rarely paid any mind to men in her proximity.

Sliding the cap from her favorite fountain pen, she began writing a list of what changes she had to make in order to feel more fulfilled with her life.

On the first line, she wrote...*"be more open to opportunities to meet a nice man."*

CHAPTER THREE

Even a blazing fire in the huge stone hearth could never dispel the coldness of the dark throne room. Gunther paced from one side to the other, the soft-soled leather boots silent on the stone floor. He had to decide, and soon, what to do next in ruling the Dark Realm. The generals and warriors would soon grow impatient. Although he was powerful enough to kill them all, inherently he was aware the darkness would not allow it.

He stopped at a long, ornate wooden table upon which scrolls and tomes were haphazardly strewn, some precariously hanging off the sides. Having scoured pages and pages, and read until his eyes drooped, he'd yet to find a way out of the current predicament. If not for dying, there was no other way to escape and return to the other realm.

Had Meliot ever felt this helpless, so desperate to abdicate that he'd consider allowing his own murder? He doubted it. Meliot's soul was dark, there'd not been one flicker of light within the evil wizard.

Outside the door, the fast speech of the guards made it known they were not happy to have been thrown out of the room. Perhaps they feared for their own lives if something were to happen to him, or they had nefarious reasons to stay informed of his every movement. Gunther suspected it could be a combination of both.

Often he read their minds to find they hated him deeply. That an interloper like him had risen to be ruler was an insult to the Torant species who were native to the Dark Realm.

Not just the guards, almost every member of the council, and every other warrior, believed him to be unworthy and wished for his death. Gunther had to agree. He wasn't from this realm, and he'd never been particularly loyal to Meliot. If anything, he'd often wished to dispatch the warlock. The only reason he had not was for fear of what had ultimately occurred. Ironic.

At hearing a knock on the door, Gunther grunted for whoever it was to enter. It was the larger of the guards, who was called Fros. Torants looked mostly human but huge, most at almost seven feet with tall, large, muscular bodies, excessively thick necks, and elongated snouts. They were a race of warriors who thrived on battle, needing little provocation or reason for violence. They were perfect, albeit unstable candidates to have in one's army.

Most of the Dark Realm's army consisted of Torants, and although Gunther had lived there for centuries, he knew little about them as the entire time he'd been held there as a prisoner, he'd given them wide berth. Especially after seeing them attack and kill other species without much provocation.

"Sire, are you to remain here?" Fros asked, his voice deep and gravely.

"What I do or do not do is not your concern." Gunther held the Torants' gaze. "I do not require your constant hovering. Go away, the both of you." He held up a hand and shot a blast of power at the guard, sending the huge creature to crash against the door. The other guard pushed the door open looking between Fros, who was getting to his feet, and Gunther.

"As you wish," Fros said inclining his head, but not before Gunther caught sight of the guard's angry glare.

The door closed behind the guards, and Gunther let out an annoyed breath. Stalking to the open balcony, he conjured a bird and sent it out with a message. Then he dematerialized, leaving behind the darkness and gloom, if only temporarily.

UPON MATERIALIZING in the outer edges of the Atlandian Realm, at the cottage he'd once lived in, it was as if heavy stones were lifted from his shoulders. He walked around the cottage, studying the structure to ensure everything was in order. Then he did the same at the stables. It was all as it should be, the roofs in good repair, the garden tidy, the stables swept. Not a whisper of another person around.

There was a groundskeeper who came on occasion, a man whom he'd hired almost a decade earlier from a nearby village. The lanky, good-natured man had never asked where he went and why he was always absent, which suited Gunther.

After being trapped in the realm for a pair of centuries, it was only in the last two decades that he'd been given enough freedom to revisit the cottage that he had first called home upon being thrust into the unknown realm.

Inspections complete, Gunther walked toward the cottage. He'd been there recently, under Meliot's orders to remove a man named Padriag. Later, he'd granted permission to the same man to find refuge there. Over the years, he'd found ways to do what he could to help men captured, but that was not something anyone knew but him and his one and only friend in the realms.

"You summoned?" Prince Sterling, ruler of the Esland Realm, walked up to him from beside the cottage. The royal's shoulder length white-blond hair blew away from his face as he regarded Gunther with a slight frown. "Be aware I will not bow to you. As far as I'm concerned you remain a commoner." The Prince's silver gaze swept over Gunther's dark attire. "Evil becomes you." The corner of his lips curved at his jest.

"As I have never bowed to you, I would never ask it in return. It is possible I am powerful enough to make you do it," Gunther teased and then blew out a breath. "I had to get away from the Dark Realm I am not sure how long I can withstand being ruler of such a place."

The prince fell in step beside him as they walked toward the woods that surrounded the cottage on three sides. "I would ask how you are finding things, but your comment says it all."

"There is naught I can do. I have scoured every tome, every parchment, hoping to figure out how to release myself from this burden. I will continue to do so, but there are eyes and ears everywhere. If they find out what I am truly searching for, it could be dangerous." Gunther stopped and concentrated to listen, ensuring he was not being spied on. "As soon as I became ruler, plans to kill me commenced."

Sterling shrugged. "Every ruler has enemies, you my friend, I venture to guess, have more than most."

They were silent for a beat, Sterling waiting to find out the reason for the summons and Gunther not quite knowing what to ask, how to seek the prince's advice.

"I need your help," Gunther finally admitted. "I read that Esland has ancient tomes with secrets of all realms."

"No," Sterling said without hesitation. "It is strictly forbidden for our transcripts to be shared with anyone not from our realm. I will never violate that law."

Anger reared, a fiery sensation surging within Gunther. It was quick and overwhelming. When he turned to Sterling, he had a tenuous hold on his fury. "I am asking for your help. Not for you to violate some law, or divulge your precious transcripts, but to perhaps find a way to help me."

Sterling took several steps backward and glanced upward where a beautiful fluorescent dragon kept watch, the creature's huge wings moving with graceful arches as it circled.

"My fire is hotter than yours," Sterling said, pointing upward.

"I would never hurt you," Gunther snapped. "I can control my powers."

"You are aware the longer the darkness dwells within the more dangerous you become. Evil will eventually win." Sterling motioned between them. "Our friendship will not last much longer."

Instead of opening his mouth to deny it, Gunther looked up to study the dragon. "She's as beautiful as she is deadly. When she destroyed Meliot's dragon, there wasn't any hesitation, as if it took little effort."

"Yes, Amai is overly protective," Sterling said following his line of sight, hands clasped behind his back. "And aye, she is deadly."

Gunther turned and they walked back toward the cottage. "You have done much for me over the years. I wish you to know I will do anything within my power to never hurt you or your people."

"Return Atlandian prisoners that have survived. A token of trust between us." Atlandia was ruled by Sterling's sisters as Sterling's realm was strictly out of bounds for anyone not from there.

At the request, Gunther stopped and looked to Sterling. Was the prince subtly offering to help him in exchange?

Gunther nodded and once again looked to the sky as Amai swooped down before gracefully landing on the ground. Her luminescent gaze moved to Gunther, distrust obvious as she lowered her giant head awaiting Sterling.

"I suggest you find one loyal subject and keep them close. You will need them at your back." Sterling climbed atop the dragon's back and met his gaze. There was something in his friend's eyes, perhaps worry, or was it pity? "I will see what I can do."

"Thank you," Gunther replied, unsure the prince could hear him as the dragon launched itself into the sky.

The suns were low, and soon Gunther would return to

the Dark Realm. There was much to do, and he couldn't afford long absences.

Once again he took in the surroundings. It was not necessarily a beautiful place, just simple, with a small field, trees, and the wooden cottage, but to live there in peace was akin to being in paradise.

Just as he was about to return to the other realm, a thought struck. Perhaps there could be a way to break free. There was a key, something Meliot had once said in passing, that had stuck in his subconscious.

"What brings death, can also be used for freedom."

Another hour of absence wouldn't hurt. At least that's what he told himself as he faded away.

CHAPTER FOUR

A choking mist blanketed everything, thick as wool and impossible to see through. Gnarled branches tore through the fog like skeletal fingers, clawing at her as she ran. The air was laced with something dark; an evil so dense it slithered along her skin, seeping into her pores no matter how fast she moved. Her breath came in ragged bursts, her feet pounding against the earth, each stride a desperate attempt to outrun the malevolent force that chased her.

She'd always been fast. But tonight, it wasn't enough. The evil was on her, its presence hot and fetid, breathing down her neck like death itself.

Then—a break in the suffocating fog. A clearing. Salvation.

Aubrey sprinted toward it, lungs ablaze, chest heaving, legs screaming in protest. She didn't care where it led only that it wasn't here. But just as she reached the edge, a crushing weight seized her shoulder. She stumbled, knees collapsing beneath her.

"Where is it? Where is the key?"

The voice, deep, inhuman, echoed around her. Over and over, the demand twisted through the air like a chant.

She jolted upright in bed, drenched in sweat, lungs still gasping for air.

And then she saw him. A man. Standing at the foot of her bed.

The silent scream rose in her throat. Her mind reeled, caught between nightmare and waking horror, as she struggled to understand:

Was she still dreaming?

"I don't mean to frighten you," a familiar deep voice said.

She saw an outline of a tall, muscled man, and blond waves that cascaded to his shoulders, his face shadowed. He shifted and the moonlight fell over him.

Dressed from head to toe in black, with a long overcoat, he looked like something out of an action movie.

It was Gunther, the warrior from the Dark Realm.

"What are you doing here?" Aubrey said, inching backward toward the headboard. She considered screaming for Padriag, but curiosity got the best of her. "Why are you here?"

His ice blue gaze met hers for a long moment, sending chills of awareness through her. She bristled with annoyance at the reaction. Even with the angry scar that ran from his left temple to vanish under the stubble of beard, he was drop-dead gorgeous.

"I require your help." He stood stock-still almost as if holding his breath. "Will you help me?"

Aubrey narrowed her eyes. "You are the ruler of darkness or something like that. Didn't you tell me you got Meliot's powers? So, no. I will not." For some reason, she didn't feel the urge to scream out for Padriag. Deep down she knew this wizard would never hurt her.

"Are you not going to ask what I need your help for? Last time we saw each other, you offered." He lifted a brow in question as if already knowing she was curious to her own detriment.

"You can tell me if you wish, but I won't do it." Something she could never resist was the urge to help those in need, hence Oscar.

Oscar.

She turned quickly from side to side, looking for her cat and not seeing him anywhere. The cat slept with her every night, dozing lazily until late morning most days. "What did you do with Oscar?"

Gunther's expression changed, hardened. The air shifted, almost stilled, and Aubrey understood he was controlling the surroundings. "Who is this Oscar?"

"If you hurt him, I will never speak to you again. Not that you care and not that I want you to ever come back..." She ran out of things to say, unable to think of anything that would threaten the huge man in the least.

When he continued to look at her in question, Aubrey let out a shaky breath. "My cat. Where is he?"

The change in his countenance was immediate. He softened and once again it was as if the air around them went back to normal. Gunther bent, standing back up with Oscar in his right hand. The cat hung like a rag doll, purring loudly, his paws opening and closing, as if kneading dough. The traitorous cat was delighted at the attention.

"I assume this is Oscar."

Before thinking better of it, Aubrey sprinted from the bed, closed in on Gunther and snatched a startled Oscar from his hand. She turned and placed the cat on the bed. It was then she realized all she wore were a bralette and panties.

Straightening slowly, she turned and lifted her chin. "Please leave my bedroom." She motioned with her hands toward the window. "Fly away, or whatever it is you do when you disappear."

Her throat went dry at noting his eyes flickered down her body before meeting hers. "It is possible that you possess something that can help me return to this world."

"What are you talking about? I don't have anything." She couldn't help remembering the voice in her dream asking for a key.

Gunther studied her for a moment. "Does your family own any old tomes, something that speaks to other realms? Your cousin, how did she come into possession of the dagger?"

Aubrey's blood went cold. No matter how he presented himself at the moment, the man before her was from the Dark Realm, an assassin and utterly dangerous.

"Is it you that keeps giving me nightmares?" Aubrey asked and searched his eyes trying to sense if he would be truthful when he answered.

Brows lowering, he seemed puzzled. "Bad dreams? I do

not believe I can affect your dreams." He seemed to be actually concerned. "What happens in these dreams?"

Aubrey was convinced he already knew, but she explained anyway. "They are nightmares. There is always a dark mist and voices asking for a key."

This time he looked away, fists clenching. Aubrey took a step backward watching his wide back as he seemed to struggle to keep calm. When he turned and looked at her there seemed to be fear in his eyes, while at the same time fury brewed just under the surface. "Can you see anyone in the dreams? Any person? Creature?" His voice sounded deeper.

Frightened, Aubrey shook her head side to side, backing up until pressing against the wardrobe beside the window. "I only see mists, feel a hand on my shoulder or my arm, from behind."

Gunther dropped his head, his wide shoulders lifted and lowered. Seeming to note that she'd moved away and stared at him wide-eyed. He moved closer and held out his hand.

"I am sorry."

Aubrey stared at the outstretched hand, then placed hers into it. The large, calloused palm closed over hers and he led her to the bed. "I will go and allow you to rest. Please consider my request."

He assisted her back onto the bed, and she slipped between the sheets, needing to cover herself from his perusal. When she looked back up at him, he was holding a picture on her nightstand. It was of her, her brother Stuart, and their parents during a holiday on the Spanish coast.

"Your family?"

"Yes," Aubrey replied. "My father Andrew, my mother, Afryea, and my brother Stuart. We went to Spain on holiday last year."

It was odd to see how gently he placed the frame back down. "You are fortunate." He met her gaze for a moment and held up a hand. Then he was gone.

She ran both hands down her face. First the dreams and then a visitor. Whether Gunther knew about the nightmares or not, he was tied to them, of that she was sure.

Despite understanding that he didn't mean any harm toward her, the fact he'd seemed to fight to keep control of his temper told otherwise. Gunther was turning into a very dangerous man.

She had to make a decision to either help him or condemn him to a life of darkness he'd never be able to turn away from.

ASTONISHINGLY, Aubrey slept soundly after Gunther's visit. When her alarm went off at seven in the morning, she stretched, a smile curving her lips, then she abruptly frowned. She'd dreamed of Gunther, that they were on a picnic in a forest clearing. In the dream they'd conversed, with her being attentive and asking about his past while fixing her plate of fruit, cheese and bread with care.

"Ugh." Aubrey pulled a pillow over her face. She considered herself much too sensible for romanticism, especially with some king of the underworld type. Of course, she couldn't control a dream that had been influenced by the late-night visit.

Sitting up, she scanned the room. In all probability, Gunther had not been there at all, only another dream. It made little sense that he would come to her for help again, especially now that, according to Padriag, he had become one of the most powerful beings in the other realm. Probably powerful enough to break free if he wished.

When she flipped the blankets off, something fell on the floor. It sounded heavy, almost like a cell phone. But a glance at the night table confirmed hers was charging. At first she didn't find anything on the rug, then a round object caught her attention. Slipping from the bed, she studied it.

A round rock, the likes of which she'd never seen, lay on the floor. Picking it up, the smooth stone fit nicely in her palm. The coloring was amazing, shades of purple blending from the darkest, almost midnight color on the edges, gradually lightening to the faintest lavender. Its beauty took her breath.

Gunther had left a gift, something to ensure she knew he really was there. And that he'd asked for her help.

"I'M DROPPING Padriag at the castle," Erin announced over the brim of her cup of coffee when Aubrey entered the kitchen after having showered and dressed in her yoga clothes. "Then I have to go to Edinburgh to work."

"Aunt Lauren has done an amazing job running things. She may be reluctant to give up her new responsibilities," Aubrey teased. "The last time I was there, she was discussing redecorating the Zen room with a woman she'd invited to class."

"I was afraid of that. She's been hinting she wants to do more than teach a class three times a week." Erin smiled. "Can you come to the studio so we can discuss things? I talked with Padriag last night about the commute from here and, later, from the castle to Edinburgh. We may want to open two additional studios, the one you want to have here in Linlithgow and one in Culross, which I can work at. Mother can run the Edinburgh studio if she wishes."

Aubrey nodded. "After morning yoga, I plan to go to the council meeting and hopefully finally get the permits approved so that I can finalize transactions for the studio here. I can be in Edinburgh about noon."

Erin gave her a bright smile. "Perfect." Her eyes shifted to the doorway, and instantly her face brightened. Aubrey didn't have to look to know Padriag had entered.

While Padriag poured himself coffee, adding milk and sugar, Aubrey steeled herself. The conversation would bring back all that they'd recently been through to rescue Padriag from the other realm. It had only been a few months, and Padriag, as well as the other four rescued men, were still adjusting to the modern world.

"Something happened last night," Aubrey blurted out and before they could respond she added, "Gunther was here."

Stunned silence followed her announcement. Erin put her cup down and looked to Padriag, who frowned at Aubrey, then looked toward the doorway.

"Where exactly?" he asked.

"My bedroom. He appeared in the middle of the night,

like a vampire, all dressed in black," Aubrey told them. "Scared the crap out of me."

Erin let out a long breath. "What did he want?" Did he threaten you?"

"What did he say?" Padriag said, his coffee forgotten as he waited for her to reply.

It took a moment for Aubrey's recollection to unscramble from the dream. "He wants me to help him escape the other realm. He wants to come here to live. He said that if my family had the dagger, we may have something that can help him."

Padriag's expression hardened. "If he has Meliot's evil within him, what he wishes to do is to come here and bring evil with him. Just like Meliot, he wants to expand the Dark Realm. You must never trust anything he says."

"He left this," Aubrey went to her work tote and pulled out the rock. Holding it out, she almost wished she hadn't shown it to them. She really liked the token.

Padriag peered at the stone. "Those are plentiful in the other realm." He didn't seem interested in it, so Aubrey put it back in her tote.

"I will speak to the others," Padriag finally said. "We may need you to come and describe all that happened. Can you come to the Dunimarle later today?"

Her day was filling up fast. "It will have to be later."

"She can come with me when I pick you up," Erin said giving Aubrey a worried look. "I pray it doesn't mean we'll be plunged into another crazy experience."

Aubrey let out a humorless chuckle. "I am not sure

about that. There is another thing." She went on to tell them about the nightmares that had plagued her for several weeks.

"And so it begins ag...ain," Erin said, giving Padriag a worried look.

Padriag nodded. "I am sure he cannot come of his own will, otherwise he wouldn't be asking for help. That is a good thing."

Aubrey wasn't sure that at the moment, anything could be described as 'good.'

CHAPTER FIVE

The Torant generals of his army, Kel and Joc, stood before Gunther with reports of observations after patrolling the realm. The older, Kel, spoke, his deep voice muffled by long incisors that grew over his bottom lip. "The Atlandians have fortified their borders. Twice the number of sentinels keep guard."

"The border to the north remains the same," Joc stated, referring to the Yorian Realm, which was inhabited by beings called Yori, that resembled the Torants, except that they were not as large and had a blueish tint to their skin. They were ruled by a Yori called Indros.

There were loud bangs on the entry door and one of his guards opened it to a warrior who hurried to where Gunther sat and lowered to one knee. "Master, you have a visitor. The ruler of Yorian approaches. He will enter the courtyard any moment now."

He hated to be called Master, but let it slide. After all, it seemed he had more pressing concerns.

"Did you know about this?" he asked the two leaders who stood before him. "How did he enter the realm without me being informed immediately?"

The Torants exchanged looks that he couldn't decipher. Upon delving into their minds, he knew that they'd hoped to meet with the Yori before Gunther was told of their arrival.

"Our scouts had not returned by the time we came to speak to you," Joc said, his expression blank.

Brushing past them, Gunther walked toward the castle entrance to greet the ruler. Whatever the Yori came to speak to him about would probably not be welcome. Although he'd never been privy to what happened when Meliot and Indros spoke, he did witness Meliot's angry rages upon the other ruler leaving.

Gunther arrived at the entrance and stood at the top of the stairs flanked by three guards on each side, the two generals at his back. More warriors, three men deep, lined up across the courtyard. Centaur-like beings were poised, bows taut, arrows notched atop the courtyard walls, prepared for any suspicious movement.

The leader of the Yorian Realm rode through the gates, surrounded by guards, albeit at a disadvantage as they were an easy target for Gunther's archers.

The Yori dismounted and, leaving his guard behind, strolled toward Gunther with the long, steady strides of a self-assured and powerful ruler, one without fear. Gunther held the Yori's gaze, unwavering. Although unsure of the reason for the visit or the ruler's intentions, he wasn't intimidated by Indros. Wearing an ostentatious golden breastplate over his tunic and a crown of the same metal, embedded with jewels on his head as well as a long deep red velvety cape that cascaded from his shoulders, Indros was the embodiment of a king.

The Yorian was tall and slender, but with wide shoulders. His skin was dark, the color of coffee. With silken, straight black hair that fell past his shoulders and bright amber eyes, the male was striking.

"I hear you wish to be called Gunther," Indros greeted. "If that is the case, you may call me Indros." He hesitated before ascending the steps and looked around, scanning the courtyard, his gaze hesitating only slightly atop the walls. Then, at flicking a finger, he magically caused every centaur to lower their bows. "I do not wish to be speared by an errant arrow today."

Indros turned to Gunther and chuckled. "They are very gullible creatures, as you may have already found."

Gunther's generals moved into formation beside him, their expressions grim, their annoyed grunts betraying their anger at an outsider controlling their soldiers. Indros' taunts were, bait, they'd failed miserably. But Gunther remained still, unaffected. He refused to give the Yori the satisfaction of a reaction.

Instead, he flicked his gaze toward the ramparts. As if in silent response, every archer shifted back into their precise positions, the coordinated movement sharp as a blade drawn. Gunther's magic threaded through their minds like steel wire, firm, focused, immune to outside influence. Even as he descended the stone steps, his power held steady, reinforcing their discipline with every stride.

At last, the two rulers stood face to face.

Indros straightened, spine rigid, clearly trying to appear taller. But even posturing at full height, he remained shorter than Gunther. Small victories.

"Welcome to my realm," Gunther said, his voice dry. He gestured toward the open archway with a slow, deliberate hand. "Please. Enter. I trust you remember the way to the throne room."

Indros' gaze swept over him, slow and assessing, as if dissecting him inch by inch. When his eyes met Gunther's, his lip curled.

"I wasn't aware you were human," he said, his voice low and laced with repugnance. "How...unexpected."

Gunther didn't flinch. Of course the Yori knew. News of his humanity had been whispered through every realm since Meliot's fall. It was an open secret. A point of weakness? Or perhaps a reason to fear. It hadn't been decided.

Instead of a reply, Gunther gave a slight nod, and he allowed the corners of his mouth to lift just a bit. "Indeed I am."

They made their way back through the same corridor, this time flanked by not only Gunther's guard team, but also Indros'.

Once inside the throne room, Indros swept his cloak around dramatically, then snapped his fingers, calling forth one of the guardsmen who removed the garment and carefully folded it over his left forearm. When Indros looked at the guard, the soldier bowed and backed away, joining the other Yori guards, who stood in a line, still as statues.

Gunther went to stand next to one of the chairs on opposite sides of a long table. The Yori ignored him and instead walked toward the window, peering out at the dark expanse.

"Interesting outcome to Meliot's demise. The late ruler hated humans from your realm as you may be aware."

"I am aware," Gunther replied. "So do most of the inhabitants of these realms."

The Yori shrugged and turned to face him. "I have never cared for what others think. I have a mind of my own. I give others the benefit of the doubt before judging."

Gunther wanted to shake his head at the male's statement, but instead he lowered to sit.

Finally, Indros deemed it time to sit. Servants brought forth trays piled with food and tankards of ale as Indros continued to study both Gunther and the surroundings. "You have not changed anything. It is all as it was or should be."

Obviously, the male was doing his best to antagonize him. If nothing else, decades as a slave had stripped him of everything, including his ability to be affected by insults. "It is not a priority. What about you? Was that the first thing you saw to upon becoming ruler? Redecoration?"

By the flare of the male's nostrils, the barb hit home.

Gunther motioned for the generals to join them on one side of the table, whilst Indros' men sat opposite them.

"I wish to speak to you about a matter Meliot and I had been discussing before his...untimely death." Indros said, lifting the tankard to his mouth and drinking.

Gunther did the same, then placed his tankard down. He spoke in a calm but steady voice. "Any agreements made between you and Meliot are no longer valid."

"It is an agreement between realms; will you not stand by it?" Indros pretended indignation.

"We can discuss it at a later date. As you have stated, I am human and therefore have a lot to learn."

"We were to join forces, fight against Esland and overthrow Sterling. Already my forces are near their northern border," Indros continued speaking as if Gunther had not said anything. "Surely you are aware of the riches within that realm."

Sterling had not mentioned the threat from the Yorians. In all possibility because the trust between them stood on shaky ground since Gunther's ascension to rule an enemy realm. The Eslandians were a formidable force. With huge war beasts called Aurocks and a fleet of dragons, they were pretty much invincible.

"The Yorian Realm is the largest. What difference would it make to invade Esland? Not to mention that my realm stands between yours and Esland. Which means, any attempts to oversee that realm would mean having to traverse through mine."

Indros gave him a patronizing look, as if explaining to a child. "Meliot understood the need for our realms to protect themselves from Eslandian invasion. Sterling is power hungry. My sources have told me he has his sights set on your realm."

It was a lie. Sterling had no interest in a realm with no redeeming qualities. Not only was the land barren, but no creatures other than Torants could ever thrive there.

Gunther kept those facts to himself and said instead, "Anyone who wars against Esland, must be thoroughly prepared. Their warriors have never been beaten in any war. A worthy opponent would have to have beasts powerful enough to battle against Aurocks, which have hides of impenetrable scales and are bred for war. Those foolish enough to attack Esland would lose a huge portion of their army to the dragons' fiery assaults, leaving their realm vulnerable to other invasions. An excellent opportunity to be overtaken, I will say."

Gunther flickered a look toward his Torant guards as he finished, noting Indros' face hardened to stone.

Apparently, Indros had not expected Gunther to know anything about Esland. Foolish thing to come into a discussion about war without knowing your opponent's strengths. It was certain, the Yori planned to take advantage of a supposed invasion and somehow unseat Gunther from his throne. Not entirely horrible, except for the fact that Gunther would never allow anyone to enslave him again.

When the male continued to be silent, Gunther lifted a tankard to his lips and took a long drink. "As I said, the conversation can wait. I have much to learn. If you are intent on our joining forces, for whatever purposes, I cannot foresee it. Personally, if I were to choose a champion in a match between a Torant and an Eslander, I would choose the latter as victor." Although his guards stiffened, they kept silent.

Indros' eyes narrowed on him and Gunther felt the intrusion, the shuffling through his mind. He almost laughed at the rudimentary attempt to not only read his thoughts but also seek a way to control him.

Lifting his gaze, he shot fiery energy pulses back at the male, who squeezed his eyes shut and gripped his head, gasping until finally able to block the onslaught. Indros was left panting, beads of sweat trailing down his temples.

The Yori glared at him, nostrils flared, lips twisted into a snarl. "You are a fool if you do not see that the joining of our realms will create an unstoppable force. I will become the greatest ruler, with or without your help. I am giving you the opportunity to share the largest kingdom, but you are a fool," Indros gritted out as he stood.

His generals exchanged looks, seeming to get satisfaction from what the Yori stated.

Gunther stood as well, following the male who stalked toward the doorway. When he let out a breath, the Indros turned to look at him with a questioning look.

Assuring a pleasant tone, Gunther spoke. "I may be a fool, but I know that if our realms ever become one, there will only be room for one ruler, which, of course means one of us would have to die."

Indros' upper lip curled into a sneer. "There is no reason for it to come to that. We are both reasonable...er, rulers."

When Gunther didn't reply, they continued on toward the opening, side by side, guards in front and behind them. It was ironic to Gunther that his men held no loyalty to him and that he could be attacked at any moment from either a Torant or a Yorian. The only thing that kept him alive was the fact that Torants barely tolerated the Yorians. Having battled against each other, their truce was a tenuous one.

IT WAS LATE when the skies were dark outside, not that it

made much different in his realm. Gunther placed his elbows on the tabletop and rubbed his eyes.

Reading through Meliot's notes for two days now and questioning the scribe who'd attended most of Meliot's meetings with others, had clarified a few things. Meliot had been cruel beyond belief, and the warlock hated Indros. It seemed he'd only agreed to a truce to keep from war with the one realm that surrounded two of the Dark Realm's borders.

The scribe, a human male, sat at a small desk that was placed unobtrusively next to a doorway that led to a study. The man, who'd been in service to Meliot for decades, had been a well-known philosopher and writer during his lifetime in the other realm. He was called Philippe, born in 1700s in Marseilles, France. The man maintained a strong French accent but was fluent in several languages.

Unlike other humans who had been captured and kept captive in the Dark Realm, Phillippe seemed content with his life. In a way, Gunther understood.

Meliot had enjoyed the philosopher's company, and they'd developed what could only be described as an indefinable friendship. The scribe had luxurious quarters and his own servants. There was little the man wanted for.

Phillippe was the only person in the realm Gunther somewhat trusted. He'd delved into the man's mind and had not detected anything other than willingness to serve.

"You do not seem to mind being here. Do you not wish to return to the other realm? To where you come from?" Gunther asked the scribe who lifted a goblet to his lips and took a delicate sip.

Philippe's eyes moved to meet his. "There is nothing left

of the France I lived in. Why would I want to return? I have seen with my own eyes the devastation of our realm over the years. No, I prefer it here."

"There has been devastation here. No realm is free of destruction."

There was a change to Philippe's countenance. An opportunity for debate seemed to brighten the man. "True. However, there is a stark difference. What happens here has not changed the realms overall. For example, this realm remains and will always be a place of darkness. No one who comes here expects anything good will happen."

Gunther walked out to the balcony and peered across the dark land. Immediately upon arriving, he himself had instantly understood that the Dark Realm was the closest he'd ever been to hell.

"You can go," he said out loud. "We will continue this tomorrow."

Once the scribe was gone, Gunther followed, down a narrow corridor and up a flight of stairs to his bedchamber. Once there, he closed the doors, leaving the guards outside.

It was as if the air became cleaner. He took in a long breath and exhaled slowly. A picture of a woman formed in his mind. A beautiful, caramel-skinned woman, with piercing brown eyes and a riot of dark curls framing her face. Her body was perfection, from the swells of small breasts high on her chest to soft curves forming an hourglass figure, her small waist flowing out to hips. He yearned to pull her to him and taste her lips, surely a delicious elixir.

Undressed he climbed into bed, his mind still on her.

"Aubrey," he whispered her name into the darkness, his hand folding over his hardened sex. "Aubrey."

CHAPTER SIX

"That is all I remember," Aubrey repeated to Padriag who watched her with an intensity that made her squirm. "Like I said, I didn't feel threatened by him. I agree, it could be a trick. Perhaps it is better if you or the other men summon him and speak to him. He may reveal more of his true intentions."

"And he has not tried to contact you again?" Padriag asked, standing and pacing in front of the fireplace.

Two days prior, she'd spent the night at the castle, too exhausted to drive after sitting with everyone there and answering question after question. By the end of the evening her brain was muddled.

"Asking more questions is only making my memory worse," Aubrey said. "If Gunther is after something that could bring him here, he won't find it. I am not going to go into grandmama's things and search for what I know is not there. Gunther is wasting his time, and you have nothing to worry about."

Erin walked to the table where they sat and handed them each a glass of lemonade. "I can see both sides. It is worrisome that he comes here. But neither Aubrey nor I know anything. Not only that, we also don't have the knowledge to practice magic. I say we leave it be for now."

Seeing Padriag's face soften at Erin's arrival, Aubrey couldn't help but smile. She met her cousin's gaze. "Thank you for rescuing me from the inquisition."

"I apologize," Padriag began, but Aubrey interrupted him.

"No need. I totally understand. Gunther took Meliot's place and Meliot entrapped you and the others. He is dangerous. If there's anything I can do to help ensure he stays where he's at, I will do it."

Padriag's grateful look made Aubrey's chest tighten, what he and the other men had gone through was unimaginable.

She went to the study to gather the necessary information for another attempt to get through to the village council and hopefully get the permits for the new studio approved. The last time she'd gone, the council had not been assembled. She and several other disgruntled people had given up after waiting for over an hour.

These were certainly interesting times.

Without prompting, a picture of Gunther came to mind.

Aubrey closed her eyes and let out a breath. Why her? Surely there was someone more adept at helping him, if indeed it was what he wanted. Unfortunately, there could only be one explanation. She had access to the others, the ones who'd escaped. He sought to harm them, and she would do anything and everything in her power to stop him.

"Aubrey," Erin stood in front of her. "You're frowning with your eyes closed. What's wrong?"

Not wishing to worry Erin, she tapped her finger on the paperwork. "I am going to meet with the village council tomorrow after my morning yoga class. Hopefully not another fruitless attempt. This is getting ridiculous."

Erin shook her head. "They need to elect younger people. The current council is made up of wonderful but befuddled older people who are not vision-forward. They want to keep things as they've always been and refuse to see that progress is not only a good thing for Linlithgow, but also inevitable."

"Maybe you should come and speak for me," Aubrey said. "I have no idea how to present it. The last two times, it was obvious whatever I said was flying way over their heads."

Erin laughed. "Let me hear your approach." Once Aubrey recited her practiced presentation, her cousin smiled widely. "Concise, straightforward and to the point. You will do great."

THE MORNING YOGA class was well attended, a perfect point to make in her presentation. She asked everyone if they minded a picture. No one protested. Then she asked a passerby to take several pictures with her phone as she posed in front of the class, sitting in a Zen position, cross-legged, feet over her thighs.

After stashing her mat in the car, she grabbed her canvas

tote and headed to where the city council was to meet in less than an hour.

The city council met in the village's community center, once a week. The group of five, all who seemed to be over sixty, were a force to be reckoned with. It seemed their response to anything brought before them by anyone younger than them was to deny the request, no matter what it was.

Steeling herself, Aubrey threw her shoulders back and strolled into the room that was marked by a hand-shaped sign with a finger pointing to the right with 'Linlithgow City Council' handwritten under it. Chairs had been set up in rows for those wishing to witness or participate in the meeting. Audrey took a seat on a chair at the end of a row, which would make it easier for her to get up and address the council.

In the front of the room, at a four-foot-long table, the council members were squeezed side-by-side. Pads of paper and a few folders scattered haphazardly on the table's surface.

The meeting began with a woman standing and reading the last meeting's minutes. Aubrey studied the council members' faces, searching for a hint of what they were thinking. Each had almost identical perfect expressions of blankness.

Finally, the minutes were done with and a council member, called Harry, held a hand up to get everyone's attention. "We will begin with past requests before hearing new ones."

Just as Audrey started to stand, Harry continued. "Unless, of course there are issues that are pressing."

A woman with a lopsided messy bun and bright red glasses perched on her nose jumped to her feet. Wearing a housedress that had to have been bought in the 1960s, the woman began speaking without waiting to be addressed.

"I believe the matter I come to speak about can only be described as pressing. It is an emergency." She swept her hands dramatically as if conducting an orchestra. "Someone is allowing their cats out at night. I could barely sleep through all the carousing sounds and then this morning I discovered two of my beautiful ceramic pots holding rare pink and purple geraniums on the ground, broken... shattered."

A man of about ninety stood up and wagged a finger at the woman. "If you will, her issue is not pressing. I would say anyone who comes to report a crime of a serious nature takes precedence."

Harry turned his attention to the older gentleman. "Do you have a serious crime to report Mr. Barthalomew?"

"Of course," the old man snapped. "I have been waiting for this meeting to report a murder."

Gasps erupted, and the old man lifted his chin as if proud to have something so urgent to report.

"Why didn't you call the police?" The woman who'd complained about the cats snapped and glared at the old man. "This is not a matter for the city council." She turned back to the front. "About the cats..."

Harry got to his feet and hurried to the older man. "Mr. Barthalomew, who was killed?"

The older man gave the cat woman a triumphant look. "Her if she doesn't stop complaining about my cats."

Laugher erupted, council members tried in vain to quiet the room and Aubrey lowered her head onto her hands. It would be a while before order was brought.

After the murder and cat commotion, a debate erupted about whether or not cats should or shouldn't be allowed to roam at night. In the end nothing was decided, except that Mr. Barthalomew was told not threaten his neighbors and keep his cats inside for the time being. Then the city council decided to postpone any more discussions until the following week.

Aubrey stood and hurried to the front of the room. Leaning on the table with both hands, she looked directly into each of the council persons' eyes. "This is my third attempt to speak to you without success. Please, I need to get my paperwork signed, otherwise, I cannot go forward with leasing the property." Since the people stared at her blankly, she quickly added. "I wish to open a yoga studio where the Darling Boutique was. I have over twenty people attending my classes in the city square. I will be providing at least four positions of employment, not counting those I hire to complete the work necessary to ensure the space is brought up to code. Additionally, Lady Whitmore has graciously agreed to report on the studio when she podcasts on the BBC channel." She was breathless, but glad to have gotten most of her practiced speech done in record time.

The council members exchanged looks seeming more exhausted than a meeting, which lasted less than twenty minutes, called for. Finally, Harry reached for the folders, sliding one after the other aside until finding hers. "I'll sign it, no need to prolong this matter."

The woman next to Harry studied her for a moment. "I do enjoy listening to Mrs. Whitmore. Very well. Ensure it is up to code and do not paint anything outside in one of those garish colors, you young people seem to favor."

Aubrey practically danced out of the room, excited about her next project. Setting up and decorating her own studio.

She'd have to call her father and ask that he contact family friend Lady Whitmore to ask for a favor since she'd made that part up.

CHAPTER SEVEN

Agonizing screams echoed, seeming to bounce off the walls. The sounds were so familiar, and yet even after decades of hearing them, he'd never grow accustomed to it.

It was expected that the ruler of the Dark Realm would inspect the torture chambers, confront those imprisoned and give orders to the guards as to how to proceed next.

When a groan sounded, the darkness pulsed through his veins, reacting to the pitiful sounds and Gunther took a deep breath at the energy that surged within. It was such a good feeling, even despite his mind acknowledging that what occurred was wrong.

He turned and walked into a dank, dimly lit room, the smell of blood and bodily fluids heavy in the air. It was rarely cleaned, the stench adding to the discomfort of those being held. A hapless man hung by his wrists. His legs had long since buckled under him. Blood dripped down his arms from where he'd struggled against the shackles in a fruitless effort to get away from whatever was being done to him.

"Unshackle him and return him to his cell," Gunther said, his voice sharp. "There are things we must discuss."

One of the torturers, a Torant with a grotesque twisted face disfigured from being tortured himself, moved to the man and unlocked the shackles, letting him collapse to the ground. His head hit with a hard thud.

Again, the darkness rose. This time Gunther pushed it down. He peered down at the unconscious man. "What was his crime?"

The other torturer chuckled. "Getting caught during our last raid of a village."

The gleeful look on the Torant's face made Gunther's stomach turn. He ruled these horrible creatures. Releasing the prisoners or stopping his subjects from committing harmful deeds would mean losing credibility and respect as a leader. The Torant race thrived on battle, destruction, torture and death.

The disfigured Torant dragged the hapless man away while the other stood next to an empty slab, another torture surface equipped with leather straps used for arms and legs.

When the Torant returned, Gunther looked to one and then the other, the entire time silent. "Your methods are rudimentary and need improvement. Perhaps practicing on one another would give you a sense of what the captives go through and how badly it really hurts. They could be faking for all you know."

Both torturers went still as statues. Gunther's personal

guards laughed, as always gleeful at the thought of pain and suffering, no matter whose.

"Fros, bring four guards here and have them perform the...new methods," Gunther stated looking over his shoulder to one of his personal guards. "Molf, come with me."

He walked away, ignoring the protests of the two who were about to be tormented.

With the guard at his heels, he went to the dungeon next. Surprisingly, there were only five prisoners being held. All seemed to be Atlandians. From the emaciated bodies on two of them, he could tell they had been there a long time.

"I'm disappointed," Gunther said. "There is nothing extraordinary done here? Do these two have any pride in their work?"

Molf grunted. "I believe they have gotten lazy. Meliot wished for there to always be captives held and they took little effort to capture the ones we have."

Gunther held his right hand out and immediately the iron door of the two cells opened. "Come out," he ordered loudly.

The males walked out, some having to be helped, including the man who'd just been tortured.

Darkness swelled inside Gunther at the pitiful sight, fighting against the compassion that made his stomach lurch. "Return to your homes. Be sure to tell others what to expect if they cross anyone from the Dark Realm. There will be no pity, ever." Lifting his hands with palms toward the group, he sent pulses of magic that would transport them back to wherever they came from.

Heavy footfalls were followed by the appearance of a Torant and another creature. Both stared at the empty cells agog. "We did not release them. It was probably the other..."

"Clean the cells until they are spotless. Once that is done, clean the corridors and once that is done, scrub the torture room. Ensure you do not disturb what is happening there." He turned to Molf. "Send guards to oversee their work."

Molf gave the jailors a triumphant look and then hurried to do Gunther's bidding.

GUNTHER WALKED from the dungeon straight out to the courtyard, needing fresh air which he gulped in lungful after lungful until finally the stench left his nostrils.

In the courtyard, there was little activity. Torants were notorious for sleeping long hours, which suited Gunther fine. Only the guards at the gates and atop the walls moved about.

The overcast sky loomed, allowing for little light. It was eternally dusk in the Dark Realm. Gunther went to the stables, planning to ride out and explore his lands. Despite living in the Dark Realm for so long, he'd never truly traveled freely and had no idea what lay beyond the few places he'd seen.

He had little to fear, his powers stronger than any other who lived in the realms. Therefore, there was no need for any kind of escort.

Mounted on a black horse, he guided the steed through the gates. Nodding to the guards who dared not question him, he continued out.

The surroundings proved to be as desolate as he expected. Gnarled trees, their branches intertwining lined the road, their branches sprouting thorns and thick grey-green leaves that could withstand the frigid temperatures of the icing.

The horse's movements seemed loud compared to the stillness of the forest. There was no birdsong, nor any type of insect about. As far as Gunther knew, the only creatures that managed to survive there were wolf-like creatures and large rodents that looked like a cross between a rat and a beaver.

Movement caught his eye and, a moment later, a deer came into view. Pulling his horse to a stop, Gunther gawked at the beautiful creature. The deer, or at least what looked like one, had thick light brown fur from the neck down to its legs. Large, doleful eyes met his for a moment, the creature seeming as startled by him as Gunther was by it.

"What are you?" Gunther asked, not expecting a reply, of course.

The sound of his voice seemed to pull the animal out of its reverie, and it whirled around and scampered away.

"Interesting," Gunther considered as he dismounted. With a long exhale, he allowed his shoulders to fall as he walked to a tree and placed his right hand against it, leaning forward, head bent.

The predicament of his current situation was over-whelming. How to maintain the illusion of continuing the way things had always been there in the Dark Realm without bringing more destruction?

In a way, it was a proper punishment that he be sentenced to life in such a place, one of no laughter, no beauty. Nothing but desolation and darkness surrounding him. He had nothing to complain about. As ruler he was not subject to mistreatment. And yet, the human in him rebelled against the notion of living in such a place, of ruling over beings that thrived on evil.

At the thought, the battle between his two halves seemed to rise, the dark rebelling against any thoughts of making changes for the better.

Without war, strife and such, what would become of the realm? There would be dissension, the Torants would rise up against him. Little prompting would be needed as it was clear none in the Dark Realm believed that a human deserved to be ruler.

Surely as he stood, back at the castle, Kel and Joc worked to find ways to dispense with him. He almost laughed. If they only knew he would gladly give up his place. If not for having to forfeit his life, he'd leave immediately.

A frosty wind blew, announcing the imminent arrival of the icing, which would overtake the realm with not only frigid temperatures, but sharp shards of ice falling from the sky. Every being in the affected areas fled to shelters, hiding from the possibility of freezing to death or being cut down by the falling icy blades.

His mind returned to the other realm, the visit with Aubrey. She'd refused to help him. Yet he knew, without her help, he could not escape. Somewhere in her reach was the key, the only way to be freed.

Of course neither she nor the others, some of whom he'd help capture for Meliot, would trust him enough to help. He didn't blame them in the least. Especially since

Gunther wasn't sure that the darkness would not follow him.

Was it fate that his penance for the past wrongs over two hundred years could only end in death?

Surely there was mercy, and he deserved it. He closed his eyes as the picture of familiar faces formed an ache like that of a hot poker being shoved into his lungs. The pain made him bend. Instinctively, he reached up and traced the path of the long, jagged scar that traveled from his left temple to his upper lip.

It could be he didn't deserve any less than the current situation. To have evil fill him and to be witness to horror and death for eternity, or until he was cut down by one of his own guards.

As the first shards of ice began falling, the horse neighed loudly, turning to look at him. Gunther created a shield to protect the animal and then himself.

Once more, he allowed his gaze to sweep over the surroundings that would soon be covered in ice, turning it into a haunted yet beautiful place.

Although reluctant to return to the stone walls of the castle, he had to. He had to continue to study the tomes and search for answers. Then he had to come up with a way to convince Aubrey that, more than anything, he wanted a chance to right wrongs and to finally be free.

His cape billowed behind as he rode back to the castle. In the periphery he caught sight of two figures hiding behind trees. Spies probably sent by Kel and Joc. The generals wished to be apprised of his movements.

The idea that they thought he wouldn't be aware was

laughable. They'd grown used to Meliot's waning powers and thankfully were not aware of how strong his were. He'd let them continue to think he wasn't aware, as it would be beneficial. Perhaps their distrust and hope to find a way to get rid of him could be beneficial in his search for a way to leave.

Urging the horse to a gallop, directing it toward the castle, Gunther's mind whirled with more questions than answers.

As he walked from the stables, the two generals stood shoulder to shoulder waiting for him to approach.

The one called Fros met his gaze, the unwavering intensity lacking any kind of due deference to Gunther's station. "We are told you released all the prisoners. As generals we should have been informed of it."

The other, Molf added, "If you could give us direction, we would assign the required duties such as cleaning and guarding to those best qualified."

As soon as the last words were spoken, the three of them dematerialized and then appeared in the throne room. Gunther on his feet, the two generals on their backs, the force of the landing taking the wind from their bodies. Both struggled until getting to their feet, their chests heaving. As soon as they stood, Gunther lifted a hand, and they were flung across the room in different directions. Furniture, tankards, lamps and all other items crashed to the floor and spilled on surfaces as the men's bodies soared past.

Molf ended up sprawled on his stomach after bouncing from the top of the fireplace, Fros slid down a wall, landing on his butt. Both growled with fury, once again getting to their feet. Molf charged Gunther, anger obviously blinding him to the fact he would not prevail against Gunther's power.

A pulse of energy sent Molf hurtling through the air, legs and arms flailing uselessly until he landed with a sickening crash atop a table that shook and collapsed. The huge Torant lay still, unable to rise this time.

Fros glared at Gunther from afar, smart enough to keep his distance.

The darkness within Gunther was gleeful, encouraging him to continue the attack, delighting in the grunts of pain and anger. He allowed it but restrained himself from continuing the punishment.

Instead, he crossed the room, found a goblet that was intact and conjured a pitcher of ale from which he poured the cold liquid. Without taking his eyes from the generals, he took a long drink.

"I must admit, this was enjoyable. I can see why Torants delight in causing pain and injury."

Molf straightened. "You disrespect our station," he growled.

"Interesting that you think that. This entire...er, interaction could have taken place in the courtyard where your men would have been witnesses."

"We are your generals, whom you should trust with..."

Gunther cut him off. "I trust no one. You must earn my trust. I am not Meliot, to whom you owed allegiance." He met the Torants' gazes. "Trust takes time."

Expressions flat, the generals exchanged looks. Gunther chose not to read their thoughts, it was obvious that they were silently agreeing to do anything in their power to find a way to dethrone him.

"Now," Gunther said, "let us sit and discuss the plans for the upcoming days." With a casual sweep of his hand, every piece of furniture and other broken items came back together, returning to their original place. All except one bowl that resettled onto the center of the table in two pieces. A reminder of what he'd done.

As soon as the discussion was over, Gunther would travel to the other realm. Time was of the essence.

CHAPTER EIGHT

Another sunny morning bathed the village park in soft sunlight, casting shadows over the soft grass. The gentle breeze carried the scent of fresh earth and blooming wildflowers, perfect for a revitalizing yoga session beneath the open sky. As the final stretch concluded and attendees rolled up their mats with satisfied smiles, Aubrey lingered behind, collecting her things with quiet contentment.

The peaceful moment was cut by a familiar voice and a blur of motion.

Zina hurried across the green, cheeks flushed, and hair tousled from her brisk walk. Dressed in yoga pants and an oversized fleece coat that billowed with every step, she was a whirlwind of mild chaos. At the end of a taut leash bounded Opal, a wiry brown mix of enthusiasm and fur who dragged Zina behind with the determination of a canine on a mission.

"Oh pooh, I knew I'd miss it!" Zina puffed, trying to catch her breath. "It's Opal's fault, she had to stop and sniff every blessed leaf on the way over. I should've just left her at home."

As if sensing her moment in the spotlight, Opal plopped down on her haunches, head tilted, ears perked, and big brown eyes fixed innocently on Aubrey.

Aubrey chuckled, crouching to scratch behind the dog's ears. "Oh, I doubt you meant to make your mum late, did you?" she said in a sing-song tone.

Opal's tail wagged, thumping against the grass with happy insistence.

Turning her attention back to Zina, Aubrey motioned to her car. "I need to put all of this away and then head to my new studio." Excitement threatened to burst from her.

"Do you want to come see the space? I'm heading to begin setting up," Aubrey told her, unable to keep the wide grin from her face. "Erin has to be in Edinburgh all week, so I'm on my own."

Zina nodded. "Which I'm sure you don't mind at all. I know how you like to start projects on your own. I'll meet you there."

With everything finally packed into the trunk, Aubrey slid behind the wheel and made the quick drive to High Street, her heart doing that strange flutter it always did when she thought about the new space. Her shop was nestled on the ground floor of a charming two-story red brick building, tucked between a bakery that always smelled like cinnamon and a florist from which she planned to purchase flowers every morning.

As she pulled up, the sight of progress greeted her. A man in paint-splattered coveralls stood on a small ladder, brushing careful strokes of sage green over the once-faded blue window frames and front door. She parked and took a moment to study the new color, calm, fresh, and elegant. *Yes*, she thought with satisfaction, *definitely the right choice.*

She grabbed a small box filled with promotional flyers and pamphlets, her hand brushing over the glossy tops, and made her way inside. The door creaked open, releasing the sharp, unmistakable scent of fresh paint.

It mingled with the subtle woodsy aroma of the exposed beams that lined the ceiling.

Inside, another painter, young, wiry, and laser-focused, balanced on a ladder as he cut in the top edge of the wall with smooth, practiced strokes. The interior shade was a soft lavender, which reminded her of the ones growing wild in the nearby hills. The muted color enhanced the exposed beams that lined the ceiling and the antique polished floorboards.

After greeting the painter, who responded with a cheerful "hello," she went directly to where the future reception desk had been set up. The wall behind it had already been painted in the palest green, which was to be used as a backdrop, a canvas waiting for the local artist to come and paint a field of lavender that would surround her new logo.

She'd spent hours with a graphic artist until finally setting on a design with the studio name "BreYea Yoga," a combination of Aubrey and Afryea, hers and her mother's names.

"This is amazing," Zina exclaimed entering. "It is absolutely perfect." She rushed past into the larger space behind the receptionist's wall.

Aubrey followed her. "I feel the same. It will be beautiful."

"I just know this is going to be a huge success!" Zina declared as Aubrey stepped up beside her, noting her friend's eyes shining with excitement.

Opal, ever the curious companion, padded across the wooden floor, her paws making cheerful little taps as she sniffed every corner like she'd been hired to approve the renovations herself.

Aubrey let out a gleeful squeal and clapped her hands. "This place just feels right. I want it to feel like a true community the moment clients walk in. I've got something special planned for everyone who signs up during opening week."

Zina pulled her into a quick, tight hug, grinning from ear to ear. "You've thought of everything. It already feels like home."

Her friend straightened and let out a long sigh, her expression unreadable. "Who has the spaces next to you?"

The question was strange, both of them had lived in Linlithgow most of their lives and knew the layout of the village quite well.

Aubrey acquiesced. "As you know, the bakery and a florist. I am not sure about the space next to the bakery, it looks empty."

"Yes, well..." Zina hesitated, "I may as well..."

"What do you think so far? Do you approve of the color?" The painter walked over and interrupted. Zina seemed relieved.

"I'd best go," she said, sailing past to fetch her dog.

After Zina left, tugging a reluctant Opal, who'd not

deemed her inspection to be over, Aubrey walked around the space with a notepad scribbling down items that she still had to purchase.

There were already boxes in rooms filled with mats, towels and other essentials. Mostly it was the smaller things that had to be procured. Decorations, office supplies and the like.

"Good afternoon," a man's voice called out from the front. He sounded familiar.

"I'm in here," Aubrey called out, waiting until the man in question rounded the wall. Her heart sank as Marcus, her ex, appeared. She let out an annoyed breath.

"Wanted to give you a wel..." His brows rose in surprise. "I wasn't aware you'd be my new neighbor."

"Wh-what, why are you..." Aubrey couldn't form words it seemed. Of all the people, he was the last person she wanted as a neighbor.

"Neighbor?" Aubrey wasn't aware that any houses near hers had sold. Not that Marcus could afford property with acres of land.

"Actually," Marcus continued, seeming to get over her surprise, "I suppose I'm also a new tenant. My permit was approved so fast, I didn't have a chance for second thoughts." Of course it was. He had a way with older women; the village council ladies had probably tripped over themselves to approve it.

Marcus was a physical therapist. They'd met when she'd needed physical therapy after a fall while hiking.

"Where exactly is your space?" Aubrey finally found her voice. "I wasn't aware any other storefronts were available."

He'd turned and walked past the front wall to peer into the interior. "Hmm, yes, well, I know the building's owner. After I told him about my wish to open Archer Physiotherapy here in Linlithgow, he offered me the space on the other side of the bakery."

As if it wasn't enough of a reminder of being dumped every time she saw Zina's fiancé. Now she'd see Marcus around the village. Aubrey stopped mid-thought. "Do Jeffrey and Zina know?"

"I had dinner with them last night."

Now she understood Zina's questions and what she had been about to say. Her friend would get an earful for not preparing her for this.

Unable to stop herself, Aubrey gave Marcus a dour look. "Why would you want to open a location here of all places. I am sure there are other villages you can charm your way into. Why here?" She couldn't keep the annoyance from her voice.

His eyebrows shot up. "I had no idea you were renting the space here. Neither Zina nor Jeffrey said anything about it."

When he didn't answer the question, Aubrey insisted. "Why are you here in Linlithgow?"

Out of the corner of her eye, Aubrey caught the painter hesitating. He was probably waiting to hear the answer too. She let out a sigh. "Well?"

"If you think this is about you...you would be right. I made a huge mistake Aubrey. An unforgivable mistake. I hope to get your trust back and perhaps one day, earn your heart again."

The statement left her stunned. Turning, she grabbed

her purse and keys and walked out of the studio, straight to her car, leaving Marcus alone with the painter.

"Never," she gritted.

ARRIVING at an empty house made Aubrey feel hollow. In the short time since Erin and Padriag had moved in, she'd become accustomed to their company.

Although Erin maintained the flat in the city, the couple had decided to live at Ashcraig Estate, since it was situated halfway between Dunimarle Castle, where Padrig spent most of his time overseeing the building of their new home, and Edinburgh, where Erin worked at the other yoga studio.

As soon as Aubrey entered, Oscar appeared winding himself around her legs and purring.

Lifting the cat, Aubrey kissed the top of his head. "Did your dispenser run out of food?" The cat managed a look of disdain as if to say the food in the dispenser was subpar.

"Very well, canned dinner for you, my lord," Aubrey said placing the cat down and walking into the kitchen with Oscar leading the way.

Once the cat began eating, Aubrey went to her bedroom. She'd shower and then work on plans for the studio. There were some orders to check on, items to order and applications to review. She had to hire a yoga instructor, which would take time to ensure she chose the perfect person.

Warm water streamed over Aubrey's skin, washing away the sweat from the day but not the questions swirling through her mind. Marcus. Two years had passed since he walked out of her life. The first, she'd wasted imagining him knocking on her door with an apology and a promise. The second, she'd rebuilt piece by piece, learning how to move forward without looking back.

So why now?

Why, after all this time, did his presence affect her? She pressed her palms to her face, letting the water fall around her.

Could she really feel anything for him now?

No. Trust, once broken, rarely healed without leaving scars. Whatever they'd once shared had been very good, but when he'd ended things so abruptly, it had shattered more than her heart. It had shattered any chance of a reconciliation.

Even the thought of friendship felt unrealistic.

It was settled. She'd speak to Marcus and ensure he understood nothing would ever happen between them and that she had no desire to ever be with him again.

Feeling better, she wrapped a towel around her body and stepped out of the bathroom stopping short, a scream erupting from her throat.

"What the hell are you doing here?" Aubrey shrieked, and without thinking she rushed forward and punched Gunther in the stomach, catching him off guard. He let out a combination grunt and gasp before stepping backward.

This was not how she pictured this day going at all. First she was to have a peaceful yoga session in the village park, followed by a delightful visit to her shop and then the day was supposed to end with a glass of wine and takeout, perhaps curry.

Only the first item on the list had gone as planned. Ignoring Gunther, she stormed to the bed, grabbed the clothes she'd laid out, consisting of leggings and an oversized long sleeve t-shirt then returned to the bathroom. "Go away," she called through the door.

Not that she expected he'd be gone. She let out an annoyed groan. What now? And why did Gunther look different? Something about his clothing.

As she expected when she walked out, Gunther remained standing, next to her bed. He held her cell phone and studied it. He wore modern clothes. Black slacks, a dark grey button-up shirt and loafers. He'd fit right into current times. Looked like most men, or perhaps not. He exuded wealth, his clothing obviously tailored to fit his toned body perfectly.

"I came to ask if you'd reconsidered my request," Gunther said, his deep voice smooth, the kind that made women take notice.

Aubrey neared and took her phone from his hand. "Even if I had any idea how to help you, I can't. For all I know you wish to come here and spread darkness. Bring the evil with you."

His chest expanded as he took a deep breath, releasing it slowly. "It is the evil that I wish to escape. The pull to lose myself in the darkness becomes stronger every day. I fear soon it will consume me and take with it my humanity."

She was mesmerized by his throat when he swallowed. "Can we talk," he asked.

"Perhaps somewhere other than your bedchamber?"

Did she have a choice? If she were to be honest, questions

bubbled in her head, there were many things she wanted to know.

"Very well." Crossing her arms, she met his gaze. "Don't push your luck and try anything. Oh, and do not take this as me agreeing to anything." Aubrey wasn't sure, but she thought the corners of his lips inched up just a bit.

They made their way from her bedroom to the sitting room. Scottish hospitality won out and she offered him a drink. Gunther nodded and she went to the kitchen, returning with two wine glasses, a bottle of red wine and a corkscrew.

Gunther took the bottle and waved a hand, the bottle uncorked on its own, the movements fluid and graceful. Then he poured them each a glass, holding out hers.

When she eyed it suspiciously, he gave her a bland look.

"It's safe. What would I have to gain by adding anything to it?"

"So many things. You can get the password to my phone; you can control my mind and make me help you..." She took the glass, deciding he could do any of those things if he wished to without tampering with her wine.

She lowered to one of two love seats, and he joined her, leaving very little space between them. Up close she could see that he looked to be about thirty. No wrinkles, the only marks were a pair of tiny lines on the outer corners of his eyes, and, of course, the brutal mark on the left side of his face. He had a perfectly shaped thin nose, full lips and sharp cheekbones. Long, dark blond eyelashes framed his bright blue eyes, the color of the Mediterranean Sea. Today his hair was brushed back from his face, the waves falling to barely graze his wide shoulders.

To sum it up, the man was breathtakingly handsome. Absently, she wondered how women had reacted to him when he last lived in this realm.

"So," Aubrey started. "Why were you taken by Meliot to begin with?"

For a long moment he was silent, a slight frown appearing between his brows. Obviously it was not an easy question to answer.

"I served as a knight in service to Stadtholder Willem, when I was taken to the Dark Realm during the Anglo-Dutch war." He studied the wine in his glass.

That was a strong conversation starter, Aubrey considered. "Where did you live before being taken?"

"The Dutch Republic, seventeen eighty-one." If he noticed she avoided asking questions about his supposed culpability, he didn't remark on it.

Doing quick math in her head, she realized he'd been in the other realm for just over two hundred years. Which made him a significantly older man. Aubrey almost giggled at her thoughts but found it impossible. Gunther emanated power, parts good, parts not. It was the latter that made her want to move away from him.

"What about family? Were you ever able to see them again?"

He shook his head, a faraway look on his face. "No. I was captive for so long, they were all dead by the time I could travel."

It was strange to sit there with a man who could snap his fingers and kill her, a man who ruled a dark kingdom of evil. And yet, despite the darkness that swirled around him, Aubrey was not afraid of him. In the deepest recesses of her being, she understood that he would never do anything to harm her.

"You said you saw me mentioned in a tome while Meliot still lived. Why do you think that was?"

He studied her, his gaze lingering on her face before falling to study her hands. "I believe because the magic knew you were to be someone that was to be an integral part of something that could affect the Dark Realm." His left shoulder lifted and lowered. "And it could be that you hold magic within that has been dormant."

"Ha," Aubrey said shaking her head. "That I sincerely doubt. If I had magical abilities, they would have surfaced when I was involved in Padriag's rescue. I was surrounded by magics and not once did I feel anything stirring."

As if doing his best to be patient, Gunther sighed and looked up to the painting over the mantel. It was an original of her great-great-grandparents on her father's side. She followed his line of sight, recalling that her departed grandmother had once possessed a magical dagger that had been instrumental in saving Padriag. Said object was also the reason why Gunther was now ruler of the Dark Realm.

She turned and looked at him. "Strange to be sitting here drinking wine with you, a man who rules an evil and dark realm. Almost like the devil." Goosebumps formed on her arms at the thought. Was this man in fact more evil than good and pretending, doing his best to trick her into doing something foolish?

Some of her doubts lifted when he looked affronted by her words. His mouth opened, but it seemed he was at a loss for words. Then he cleared his throat and frowned. "I can see why you think that. It's understandable."

"Another question," Aubrey began. "What exactly do you think will free you? And what would you do if freed?"

"Those are two questions," Gunther clarified with a smirk. "I am certain you hold the key. Otherwise, why were you in Meliot's book? I am not sure what I would do, or where I would go. The Dutch Republic is no more."

Aubrey stood and walked to stand next to the fireplace. "I can't help you. A part of me believes that you are sincere in wishing to be freed, to leave the other realm. However, there are too many reasons as to why I should not."

As if measuring his movements, he stood to his full height, which she guessed to be perhaps six-four. Then, before she could stop him, he stood in front of her. He took her right hand in his and placed it flat on his chest over his heart. Solid chest, Aubrey considered, the steady thudding of his heart under her palm steady.

He met her gaze. "On my honor as a knight of King Wilhelm, I swear that I only wish to be freed. I will do no harm to you or others."

When their gazes clashed, Aubrey searched the blue depths. Was he as honest as he appeared to be? A knight never violated an oath made. At the same time, the darkness within Gunther could push past any honor.

There was no evidence of anything other than sincerity and the darkening of his eyes was not evil, but something else. Desire.

Realizing how close she stood, with her palm flat against his muscular chest, Aubrey pulled her hand free. They stood so close, she could smell the woodsy aroma and something clean. She wanted to sniff to be sure, it smelled as if he'd used a very expensive shampoo or body wash.

Her wits were rattled, Aubrey thought as she moved away, turning to face the large windows that overlooked the back gardens. "I am not promising anything. But I will search through my grandparents' things in the cellar. Perhaps there is something there. Although I do doubt it, so don't get your hopes up."

She turned to look at him. The man was gorgeous, which made him even more dangerous. It was impossible, at least for her, to not feel the pull of attraction.

"That is all I ask," Gunther said, lowering and then lifting his gaze to meet hers. "Do not be afraid of me."

Of course she was afraid of him. The man ruled a realm known for death and torture. It certainly would be foolish to let her guard down.

"I am not afraid, but uncertain of you," Aubrey replied. "How can I not be?"

He moved closer, not stopping until she could easily reach out and touch him. He slid a glance sideways as if deciphering what to say. It was almost as if he was nervous, uncertain, like a teenager about to ask a girl for a first date.

She let out a huff, annoyed with herself. "What is it?"

Finally, he met her gaze. "Do you...er, are you in a relationship?"

Aubrey blinked in surprise at the question. "What?"

"I mean," he quickly added, "it could make for complications."

"Complications?" Aubrey let out a breath. Not waiting for him to say anything else, she quickly said, "I am not at this time, not that it any of your business."

The corners of his lips inched up just a bit. "I am glad to hear it."

Gunther leaned in and pressed a soft kiss to her lips. It was brief, teasing, just enough to make her breath catch and her body react. Whether it was meant to be romantic or not, he'd just lit a bonfire.

Aubrey grabbed the front of his shirt and yanked him closer. His eyes widened just before she rose onto her toes, looped her arms around his neck, and kissed him with a hunger that had been building for too long.

Their mouths collided in a passionate tangle, no hesitation, no holding back. His arms came around her like instinct, crushing her against the hard, unyielding planes of his body. There was definitely chemistry because the heat between them flared instantly.

She deepened the kiss, her fingers threading through the soft strands of his hair, claiming him. His low growl vibrated against her mouth and sent a delicious shiver down her spine.

Every inch of him was muscle and heat and need. And every part of her wanted to touch all of it.

When his hands slid down her back, slow and deliberate, she let out soft moan and dragged her fingers along his muscled arm. He was trembling. So was she. Whatever this was, it wasn't a kiss anymore. It was the start of something dangerous. Something inevitable.

And heaven help her, she wanted more.

"Aubrey!"

The voice was like a splash of icy water jolting her out of the moment. It was as effective as a bucket of icy water, and just as shocking.

She shoved Gunther away, breathless and dazed. He stumbled back a step, his broad chest heaving and turned to the doorway.

"Oh...shit," Aubrey whispered, eyes locking onto her cousin.

Erin stood in the doorway, wide-eyed and stiff with disbelief, her mouth slightly open as if she were still trying to process the scene before her. Her arms crossed slowly, deliberately, as she shifted from stunned observer to judgmental witness. The look on her face made Aubrey feel sixteen again and caught kissing a boy behind the school.

She glanced at Gunther who, infuriatingly, managed to look both guilty and impossibly gorgeous. His face was flushed, though whether from passion or embarrassment, she couldn't tell. His tousled hair looked like she'd run her hands through it, which she had, and a smudge of her lip color curved along the edge of his mouth. He looked completely ravished.

It might have been funny...if he weren't the literal Prince of Darkness.

"You should go," Aubrey said quickly, smoothing her hair and trying to gather what little dignity remained. "I'll explain to my cousin what we discussed."

But Erin's eyes narrowed, lips pursed like she was channeling every furious matriarchal ancestor. "Oh no," she said, voice clipped and authoritative. "He stays. *Both* of you are going to explain what exactly is going on."

Gunther cleared his throat and straightened, though the pink stain on his lips betrayed any attempt at regality. Aubrey sighed. There was no easy way out of this one.

Both she and Erin watched as Gunther straightened, shoulders back. "I am here to once again ask Aubrey for help in leaving the other realm." He cleared his throat and slid a glance to her. "I have given her my oath that I would not hurt anyone or bring any darkness to the realm."

"Are you prepared to speak to the others? Tristan, Gavin, Niall, Ian and Padriag?" Erin asked tapping her foot. "They are better suited for this than Aubrey. Neither my cousin nor I have any experience in helping you or anyone."

"Once the key is found I will return." With one last glance in her direction, he dematerialized, leaving behind the expensive scent and Aubrey's rattled senses.

"OH. MY. GOD." Erin repeated, pacing in the kitchen as Aubrey poured a tall glass of cold water and drained it, her heart racing and body pulsing with desire the entire time.

"I don't know what came over me," Aubrey said covering her mouth with both hands to hide the fact that for some stupid reason she kept smiling.

Erin huffed. "He took advantage, plain and simple."

"Actually...I kinda grabbed him. I mean, he did kiss me first, more like a peck. It was sweet...but when he made to leave...I sort of attacked him."

Her cousin blinked. "Why would you do that? He's

going to become very evil, even if he isn't yet. Padriag says, he is powerful and able to do much more harm than Meliot."

"I always did like the bad boys," Aubrey quipped, attempting to lighten the moment.

To her relief Erin relaxed and nodded. "True. But he is as far from a boy and way more than bad."

"You can say that again," Aubrey said letting out a long sigh.

CHAPTER NINE

E ven the dimness of the castle didn't diminish the lightness in Gunther's chest as he observed the proceedings. Two days since returning from the other realm and still he could feel the softness of Aubrey's body against him, the feel of her plump lips against his. Each time he inhaled, he expected the aroma of wildflowers that had clung to her hair.

The woman was like none other he'd ever been with. Her cinnamon skin, dark brown eyes and full lips could drive a man mad. She was tall, perhaps five foot eight, a perfect fit against him as he was well over six feet. Then there was her hair, a riot of soft curls that ranged in colors from golden to rich brown. Everything about Aubrey was a siren to his senses.

"Do you agree with the punishment," Kel, one of the generals brought him back to the present.

Two Torant warriors were being punished for the brutal

beating of another warrior who, according to the accused, had annoyed them.

"Yes," Gunther said, not caring what Torants did to one another. The species seemed eager to find any occasion for fighting and warring. The accused, who looked as if they'd already been punished, were dragged out and the darkness within him seemed to come alive at the sight. Thoughts of watching the torture gave him a surge of pleasure at what he was about to witness.

As long as he was able, he wouldn't succumb.

He looked to the generals, behind them four guards each. "What else?" he growled, annoyed that they pretended what he said was worth anything. They would do whatever they wished regardless of his orders. Unless he interfered, which he didn't care enough to do.

"Bring in the prisoner," Joc ordered.

A Yori was half carried in and dropped to the stone floor. He lifted his head and spat at Gunther. No one in the room said anything or stepped forward.

Gunther waved a hand sending the prisoner and the two guards who'd brought him in rolling across the floor, landing in three heaps.

"Why is the Yori here?" He turned his attention back to the generals.

The generals watched the guards stand and once again bring the Yori forward, this time not as close to Gunther.

"He was caught at the border between our realms. Part of a patrol."

"It is expected. We do the same," Gunther said in a bored tone. "What made your warriors decide to take him?"

"They were overheard talking about an upcoming attack on our realm." Came the curt response. "He was brought to be questioned."

Gunther looked to the prisoner and delved into his mind. Mostly he was thinking about escape and his impending death. When he went deeper, the fact the Yorians were indeed planning to attack became clear.

"Do not kill him. Allow him to heal from his wounds but give him no healing treatments. Food and water, to keep him alive. We may be able to use him as a bargaining chip."

The prisoner was taken away.

All others were dismissed except for Gunther's personal guards and the two generals.

Joc spoke first. "We must fortify our borders. Multiply the number of Torants patrolling."

"Already we have defense stations," Kel added. "They will be manned at all times. But we need more warriors."

Gunther gave them a droll look. "In other words, you are doing now what you should have been doing all along."

The generals barely managed to restrain their anger, their nostrils flaring in annoyance, glares directed past him as they were not stupid enough to disrespect him directly.

"After the battle with Esland and the humans, our numbers were depleted. Master, you have not conjured additional fighters. And although we've recruited additional Torants, the numbers are still not where our army should be."

Gunther stood and walked down the two steps from his throne, which he found pretentious, but nonetheless used to assert his station. "I do not recall either of you briefing me about the army's numbers. As you are aware, I am not Torant and, although living here for many years, I was not privy to such information."

The Torants were silent, unable to defend themselves against the truth.

"Go. Return tomorrow with information as to the army's strength. I wish to know who was killed or is missing. Names of Torants and numbers of the conjured, if they had any."

"Yes, Master," both generals agreed in unison. They called him Master, not out of respect, but because they knew he hated it.

The generals turned to go, but he stopped them. "And... stop calling me Master. I am Gunther."

PHILLIPPE JOINED GUNTHER FOR DINNER. The one thing he enjoyed since becoming ruler was the delicious meals. This night, there were thinly sliced beef in gravy, red potatoes and roasted vegetables, accompanied by steaming buttered rolls.

Meliot had brought livestock and other necessities from the other realm so that he could eat as if he were still there. The one and only thing he was grateful to Meliot for.

"How was Meliot's relationship with the generals?" Gunther asked as he cut into the meat.

The scribe chewed his food before replying. "I would say they tolerated each other. Meliot rarely agreed to anything the generals proposed, often preferring to oversee the warriors himself. Battle plans were his and, as you know, he personally oversaw any questioning and punishment of prisoners."

"It would seem the generals would relish a ruler who gives them more freedom." Gunther speared meat and potatoes onto his fork, eating the bite with relish.

"Torants are not the kind to relish anything," Phillippe replied, matter-of-factly. "Quite the opposite. They thrive in disagreements and chaos."

Gunther nodded. "So I have noted."

"They plot to kill you," Phillippe said in a light tone, as if it was non-consequential. Then again in that realm, it was probably the norm. He already knew the Torants had planned Meliot's demise regularly.

"I am not surprised," Gunther replied. "How successful do you suppose they will be?"

Phillippe shrugged. "As long as you are so powerful, it will prove difficult. I tell you because if you die, then I will be of no use to the Torants. They only tolerate me because Meliot protected me and now, you seem to as well."

The scribe could prove useful, Gunther thought. However, he wasn't foolish enough to confide in the man or trust him fully. For all he knew, Phillippe could be turned to betray him if tortured by the Torants. It was best to let the man think he trusted him.

"If you know this, why not ask to be returned to the other realm?"

The man shrugged. "You remain quite powerful. There is little that can destroy you. For now."

For now.

Gunther decided to table the subject of his demise for the moment. "Did Meliot have any plans for the Yorian Realm? I didn't see anything in the tomes you provided."

"If he did, he never told me or had anything recorded. I was banned from the room whenever Indros was here. No one except Meliot's and Indros' personal guards remained with them."

Interesting. Meliot's personal guards were killed the same day that Meliot was dispatched.

"Why do you suppose that was?"

Phillippe placed his silverware down carefully. "Because they both plotted to destroy one another while pretending to be working towards a union. After one of Indros' meetings, I entered the room preparing for the briefing to the generals. It was just Meliot and I. His guard was down. He blurted that Indros thought him a complete idiot, that he knew the other ruler's plans to conquer this realm."

Gunther wondered why Indros had not taken advantage of Meliot's weakened powers to strike. "Indros was more powerful than Meliot in the end."

"Yes, he was. But Meliot used up all his strength, making a show of power during the visits, even if it left him weakened for days after."

"Were the generals aware of his weakness?"

Phillippe shrugged. "I do not think so. Meliot was a master of deception. His powers came and went. When strong he sent for the generals."

They ate in silence for a long moment.

"Can you travel to our native realm?" Gunther asked a startled Phillippe, whose eyes widened as he lifted his left wrist. A magically conjured band around it was so tight, it was embedded into the man's skin.

"I cannot," Phillippe replied. "I am not sure that, even without this, I know how."

Gunther studied the bracelet for a moment, then removed it, the object disappearing, leaving a visible indentation in Phillippe's wrist.

"No need for that," Gunther said. "If you wish to return, you can. I prefer not to keep captives from our realm against their will."

"There is nothing for me there," Phillippe stated, his eyes locked to his arm. "Where would I go?"

Gunther shrugged. "Decide and I will help you get established. The darkness is gaining power in me. Soon I will not be inclined to generosity."

"I will remain for now. When the time is right, I will leave." Phillippe's reluctance was understandable. Gunther himself wasn't sure what he'd do if Aubrey was ever able to help him escape permanently. After centuries away, living in a completely different world, the idea of a normal life seemed a fantasy.

"How was it you ended up here?" Gunther asked the scribe.

For the first time since meeting him, Phillippe's face hardened. "Defending my family. I gave myself as a slave to Meliot in exchange for him sparing their lives."

"And yet you never seemed to be resentful of him."

"I was in the beginning. After many years, I came to accept that he stuck to his part of the bargain. He treated me fairly."

Gunther shook his head. "Nothing about Meliot was ever fair."

The man studied him for a long moment. "I do not expect you would share your story."

Measuring his words, Gunther gave a noncommittal shrug. "Like you, I made a reckless bargain with the devil."

There was no question or judgment in the scribe's demeanor as he began to eat again and in that moment, Gunther was envious of Phillippe. Unlike him, the man was not wracked by guilt over the circumstances that brought him there.

DUTCH REPUBLIC 1784 DURING THE ANGLO-DUTCH WAR

Gunther drove his sword deep into the man's gut, the blade sliding between ribs and sinew with sickening resistance. For a heartbeat, time seemed to freeze, the enemy's face twisted in pain and disbelief, his blood soaking Gunther's hand where it gripped the hilt. This wasn't just another kill. This man had taken one of Gunther's closest friends not moments before.

A guttural scream ripped from the dying man's throat as he thrashed, trying to pull himself free, clawing at Gunther's arms with failing strength. But Gunther didn't let go. He shoved the blade in farther, twisting viciously until the man's eyes widened and then dulled. A shudder passed through the body before it slumped forward, lifeless.

There was no time for satisfaction.

A shadow loomed, hooves thundered, the sharp whoosh of descending steel a sound a seasoned warrior heard. Gunther yanked his sword free and pivoted just in time to parry a brutal claymore strike from a mounted warrior. Sparks erupted from the clash, the sheer force jolting through his arms and nearly sending him to his knees.

All around him, chaos reigned. Screams of dying men mingled with the metallic rings of blades striking blades. Horses reared and shrieked, their panicked cries tearing through the battlefield like a chant. The stench was overwhelming, the unmistakable smell of coppery blood thick in the air, mixed with the rank stench of sweat, bile, and death. The ground had turned into a mixture of mud and gore, slick beneath his boots, unforgiving and treacherous.

Bodies littered the field, some groaning, others grotesquely still. And those who were slow to rise risked being crushed beneath thundering hooves, their cries snuffed out in a sickening crunch of bone and armor.

Gunther's heart pounded in his chest like a war drum. Blood ran into his eyes, hot and sticky, from a blow he hadn't even seen coming. His vision swam. The edge of the world blurred. Every movement took more effort, every breath felt heavier. Whoever had struck him had done damage.

He could feel it in the marrow of his bones; he and his men were outnumbered. Severely. The line would not hold much longer.

And if it broke...there would be no one left to bury them.

The British were going to win; Gunther had no illusions otherwise. The Dutch Republic was undergoing civil unrest; the country divided between those loyal to Prince William of

Orange and those opposing. Factions against the ruler, called Patriots, were rapidly gaining popularity.

The Republic's army was fighting on two fronts. Against the British over the Dutch helping the American colonies, and in the revolution between the loyalists and the Patriots.

To further weaken the army, the Dutch Republic fought against the powerful British forces on both land and sea.

A hard blow came from somewhere overhead, and he was sent rolling several feet over bodies and dirt, landing with a hard thud on the blood-soaked ground. His head swam and vision blurred, he fought to get up to all fours only to fail when something heavy fell over his back, pinning him to the ground.

It was a horse who'd fallen sideways. By the lack of movement, the steed was dead and soon he would be too, his ability to breathe almost impossible.

Gunther's vision cleared and he saw that his men continued to fight valiantly, one a young man called Durst, who'd recently married, stumbled backward from a hard strike, let out a yell and surged back into the fold.

Despite his predicament, pride filled him watching his countrymen fight a losing battle with honor.

Darkness began to envelop the field and the sight before him faded behind a mist, all sound and movement ceased, the battlefield frozen. Was this how death came? Gunther wondered.

A figure emerged from the thick fog, human-like with long black robes. Gunther prayed that it didn't mean he would spend eternity in hell. Other than in war, he'd strived to spend his entire life doing what was right. Yet perhaps it hadn't been enough.

As the figure neared, Gunther realized the horse was gone, all pain gone, his body seeming to relax. It had to be the coming of death.

"If you wish to save your men, give yourself freely to me." It was a man in the robes, a sort of demonic apparition, by the way something like lightning bolts burst from his fingertips. "I can make this all go away, rescue your men, give you safe harbor. All you have to do is pledge fealty to me."

The visitor's glowing eyes dug into his. There was an air of impatience as he snapped his fingers to get Gunther's attention. "You are dying. It is a simple decision. Save your men, serve me or you and your men perish today."

He didn't care what happened to him; however, he didn't want the men he'd led to die. Those who had power sent them to fight a losing battle they barely understood while sitting back drinking wine and feasting on fatted pigs.

"I will serve you," he replied in a hoarse voice. "Save them."

The battlefield came into view again. Suddenly the enemy retreated, turning their horses and selves away.

What happened next, Gunther didn't understand. Every Dutch soldier stood still as statues, the wizard walking among them, looking into their faces as if trying to identify them. He touched one on the shoulder and the man fell dead.

"No." Gunther could barely speak, his lungs burning with the need to breathe.

"Ah yes, I forgot," the wizard's voice sounded in his head as the horse once again disappeared.

"Wh-what are you doing?" Gunther struggled to all fours. "Do not kill them."

"I am called Meliot," the wizard said in a calm voice.

"*That man was dying.*" *He continued his walk, touching a man here and there until several collapsed to the ground.*

"*Now, your new life begins.*" *The wizard's smile sent shivers down Gunther's spine.* "*Your men will not live long, many of them will perish in the next war. You are only prolonging the inevitable.*"

"*No.*" *Gunther got to his feet, swaying as if drunk.* "*You said you'd save them.*"

The wizard chuckled. "*I did. And you will obey me.*"

"*Not unless you keep them safe.*"

The wizard looked at the young warrior Gunther had been watching earlier, touched his shoulder and Durst fell to the ground. He was dead.

Gunther bent, took a sword and rushed toward the wizard. "*I give myself to you,*" *he cried out.* "*Do not hurt them.*"

Now the wizard bent and touched Durst. The young fighter sat up looking about with confusion.

Meliot then waved both hands, sending Gunther into a tunnel of spiraling lights. It was as if he fell down into a void. There was no sound except for his gasps and attempts to keep from vomiting as he floated past swirls of lights that streaked past.

Finally, he landed on hard ground, the wind knocked from him. When he stumbled to his feet, he lost the contents of his stomach.

After a moment two things struck him. First he was fully healed, except for his unsteady belly, and secondly, wherever this was, he was no longer in his homeland.

The sky was a strange shade of purple with swirls of lights and there were three moons of various sizes overhead. One so large it was as if he could reach up and touch it.

Tall black trees with twisted trunks and spindly branches formed a forest of sorts. There was no grass on the ground, instead it was covered in a thick grey moss.

At the sounds of grunts, he turned around and stumbled backward. Huge, muscular beings who looked almost human, except for an elongated nose and mouth like that of a wolf or dog, stood in a line studying him intently.

Not only was he no longer in his homeland, but it seemed he was no longer in the same world.

"Is THERE anything else you require of me today?" Phillippe's question brought Gunther out of reminiscing. Obviously the man understood he was not going to share how he'd ended up in the Dark Realm.

"No, you may go."

Gunther pushed the food away, his appetite gone as a strange sensation overtook. Someone was calling for him.

CHAPTER TEN

When Gunther materialized in Scotland, the world came into sharp, vivid focus. He didn't move—not because he was afraid, but because something held him fast. Looking down, he found himself encircled by a glowing ring of salt and glinting gems, a containment spell drawn with meticulous care. Yet, before he even acknowledged the figures standing nearby, he closed his eyes and drew in a deep breath. The air was rich and alive; warm sun on fresh grass, the earthy trace of moss, and a trace of sea salt carried on the breeze from the nearby shore. It was the scent of freedom, and yet he was bound.

Upon opening his eyes, he noted he was within sight of Dunimarle Castle. Looking from side to side he took in the men who surrounded him.

Four of the knights, who'd recently escaped the other realm, stood with a variety of weapons that, like them, spanned the centuries.

Tristan and Padriag held swords, whilst Niall McTavish

and Liam Murray stood with feet apart, pointing guns at him. Gavin was missing, probably away and unlike in the other realm had to rely on the slower modes of transportation.

"You summoned?" Gunther asked in as calm a voice as he could muster while pushing back the dark powers that surged at being restrained. Despite being quite powerful in the other realm, he wasn't sure to be as able here.

It was Tristan McRainey who spoke for the group. "Why have you appeared to Miss Macguire twice and asked her to help? Why would you require help from anyone?"

Past Tristan he noted movement at one of the windows. It was too far to see clearly, but undoubtedly, it was the men's partners keeping watch. Was Aubrey with them? He ached to see her face, to hear her voice encouraging him. At this moment he was utterly alone.

"I asked you a question," Tristan insisted.

Gunther met the man's gaze. "I am fighting to leave the other realm and return to this one. I am bound by Meliot's magic to the Dark Realm and cannot break free on my own."

A huff got his attention and Gunther looked at Liam. The knight's disdain was evident in the curl of his upper lip. "I sense darkness. You reek of it. What you wish to do is to spread evil here."

No matter what he said, the men would never believe him. He didn't blame them, for centuries they'd been mistreated, tortured and tormented by his predecessor.

"I admit that I do not deserve the benefit of the doubt. As it stands, the only way for me to be released from the throne is by death."

There was silence as he was sure the men all thought his death was not altogether a bad thing.

"I want to return home. If I am to die, I wish it to be here." Gunther looked up to the sky. "I am aware there is naught a way to convince you that I wish to bring no harm to this realm."

Niall spoke next. "You are correct in that. Return to the darkness from which you came and stay there. Do not bother Aubrey again."

"You should guard her," Gunther said earning glares all around. "She should be kept safe, not from me, but from whoever succeeds in dethroning me. Aubrey is named in Meliot's tomes."

Gunther decided to try one last-ditch effort to convince them of his wish to return to a normal life. He directed his attention to Padriag, the one who he'd help rescue.

"When I helped you, I was not aware of the ramifications, that as the only person present I would absorb the wizard's powers. I was prepared to stay in the other realm; I deserve no less. However, I do not wish to be fully consumed with the evil that lurks within me now and become overcome by the darkness. That I do not deserve." He held Padriag's gaze. "I need your help. Please."

The allusion to the young knight being indebted to him was left unsaid, but he sensed the man was moved, even if a miniscule bit.

"Even if you are being honest, there are no guarantees that the darkness that resides in you will not follow. Am I right?" When the others grumbled at Padriag's words, he held a hand up and pinned Gunther with an intense look. "You do not know the answer to that, do you?"

The man was right. Gunther let out a long breath feeling a heaviness push down on him, the sickening voices rising in his head.

"Kill them. Kill them. It will feel so good. You will delight in it. Kill them."

A heady sense like that of eating the most delightful morsel, of being pleasured, of gentle strokes all over his body felt wonderful and he almost moaned at the evil's teasing. Summoning strength, he pushed it away and let out harsh breath, his jaw tight.

"No, I have no knowledge if my freedom will bring with it destructive consequences or if I will be able to live a normal life," he replied.

There didn't seem to be any softening in the men's expressions and Gunther felt defeated. He lifted his hands and lowered them in a motion of giving up.

They would not help them and in all probability would keep Aubrey from him as well. He didn't blame them, if she were his, he would die before allowing someone like him, a man destined to cruelty and madness anywhere near her.

Testing the circle's hold, Gunther pushed against the invisible walls. Although the magical hold was strong, he was sure he could escape it. He didn't try, instead, waited for whomever would come, curious to know if Aubrey would be among them.

STANDING AT THE WINDOW, Aubrey could not tear her gaze from the view. Although the sash was open to allow for a breeze to blow in, it was impossible to hear the discussion.

In the center of a magical circle, feet planted wide, and shoulders squared, Gunther looked every bit a Viking warrior. The subtle wind blew through his hair, the blond strands playing across his shoulders.

He was unarmed from what she could see, no sword across his back or dagger at his hip. Despite it, she was not fooled. He was lethal and could probably free himself from the magical hold. That was, if his powers worked in this realm.

"What are they saying?" Tammie, Niall's wife, asked, shifting from one foot to the other impatiently.

"Shhh," Gwen, Tristan's wife, hissed leaning forward. "They are telling him something about not helping 'cause they don't trust him."

Aubrey looked to Erin, who shrugged. "I can't hear anything."

They turned their attention back to the group of men who continued to hold their weapons at the ready in case Gunther tried anything.

He was darkness and evil, Aubrey reminded herself. Still, the memory of being in his arms, of his mouth over hers overtook all common sense, making it impossible to believe he meant harm.

"Look," someone said, and she snapped from her thoughts to see that Padriag and Gunther were having an exchange. Padriag held a hand up and said something to Gunther.

As if in defeat, Gunther held both hands up and lowered them. Her chest tightened, a part of her hoping that they did the right thing. If Gunther had evil plans, then they were saving their homeland. However, if he was truthful and only wished to be freed, then how to live with that?

"I need to speak to him." Aubrey sprinted from the room ignoring the alarmed calls from her cousin and the other two women.

Once outside, with them on her heels, she hesitated only for an instant, then sprinted toward the men, who hadn't noticed her.

Gunther was the first to see her, barely giving any indication. Probably hoping she'd make it close enough and plead his case.

However, at the sound of the women calling her name, the other men all turned to look at her.

Padriag lowered his sword and held up one hand, palm toward her. She took two additional steps and bounced backwards, hitting an invisible wall.

"I need to know the truth!" She met Gunther's gaze and screamed. "Why is my name in those books? Why are you really here?"

The women caught up to her. Both Gwen and Tammie moved to stand in front of her, but Aubrey pushed them apart. "Answer me."

Looking first to the men, as if asking for permission, Gunther waited until Padriag nodded before replying. "I cannot read the ancient language of the realm. The Scribe translated that you are too lethal to the ruler of the Dark Realm."

"Why?" Aubrey asked, her gaze taking him in. How a man could be so beautiful when holding evil within was alarming. His long lashed blue eyes narrowed as if trying to figure out what she was thinking. Aubrey almost cringed.

"I cannot answer you. I do not know."

"Enough," Tristan interrupted. "Return to the Dark Realm and do not come back."

Gwen and Tammie held hands, prepared to chant the spell that would prompt his departure.

"I cannot promise not to return. I will continue to fight to be free." Gunther dematerialized, leaving no trace that he'd ever been there.

The magic circle had not held him. He'd chosen to remain to plead his case and to not harm any of them.

"WHAT WERE YOU THINKING," Erin chastised Aubrey for what seemed like the hundredth time. "He could have grabbed and taken you." Worry lines crisscrossed her cousin's face.

Aubrey shrugged. "He was in the circle."

Everyone was inside the castle, sitting around a long table in the dining room. The men were mostly silent, seeming to be organizing their thoughts before speaking. The women were not as patient.

Gwen gave Aubrey a droll look. "You do understand he could have broken from the circle at any time right? By the way he dematerialized, it is apparent he stayed in place of his own will."

"What does that say?" Erin asked. "Is it a trick? Something he did to manipulate us into thinking he is being honest?"

"If he is anything like Meliot, then yes." Tristan let out a breath. "What he states is not of import. What worries us is his claim that Aubrey is named in Meliot's tomes."

"Is there something you can do? Some sort of magical protection to keep Aubrey safe from him?" Erin looked on the brink of tears. "I have been there, and it is horrifying."

Tristan rapped his knuckles on the table getting everyone's attention. "Although I doubt most of what Gunther stated, I do believe Aubrey is in danger. Any ideas on measures to keep her safe?"

"We'll have to go through things that belonged to your grandmother and see if there is anything that could possibly be used against you," Gwen said.

Liam added. "The dagger was in your family's possession; there has to be a reason why. There could be other things." His ice blue gaze moved between her and Erin. "Where would her things be?"

It was Erin who spoke next. "We can search the cellar at Ashcraig House," she suggested. "There are heaps of things stored there."

"That's a good idea," Aubrey said. "Nothing else occurs to me. If it comes to it, I will speak to Da and ask if he has any other items of interest," Aubrey quickly added. "Although that would be the least preferable thing to do. He is very inquisitive and will ask tons of questions."

Aubrey blew out a frustrated breath. "When I asked Da about grandmother, he told me she was a collector of items that she considered to be used in medieval magic. Also, that she was casual about it, as if she didn't quite believe in their powers, but liked the idea of it."

"Aubrey and I will start the search right away," Erin explained. "It is not a large space, so we should be able to handle it. I will ask for help if it is needed."

"Meanwhile, Tammie and I will research protection wards for both the house and both of you," Gwen said as the others around the table nodded their approval.

There wasn't much more that could be done, and in all honesty, the more pressing matter at the moment was opening her studio. Already notices had been sent to the local newspaper and preparations made for the grand opening in less than two weeks. The amount of work that was yet to be done made her head spin.

"It will all have to wait for a couple weeks. As you may all remember, I have to be prepared for my yoga studio's opening. I cannot be spending hours in a smelly cellar."

They discussed how everyone had tasks at hand, from helping Aubrey with her studio to overseeing the building of homes on Dunimarle lands.

Finally, they deemed that Gwen and John, Liam's partner, would work on the wards to keep Aubrey and Erin safe.

Aubrey let out a long sigh. She'd been counting on Gwen and John's help for the studio, but at the same time, she understood that if she were snatched and taken to the Dark Realm, her life could be in danger.

And yet, she wasn't afraid of Gunther. Her gut instinct was that he would never harm her.

CHAPTER ELEVEN

THE YORIAN REALM

Generals Joc and Kel urged their nervous, wooly steeds forward across the top of a narrow ridge. In front and behind, their Torant escorts formed a single row. There was no room for protection on their sides for fear of falling to a deep chasm, a combination of jagged rocks and swirling waters. Steam from the water below rose, forming a hazy fog that added to the rather strange beauty of the surroundings.

This realm was nothing like from whence they came. It was composed of what looked to be floating islands connected by bridges constructed of a white claylike substance. Looking closer, it became evident that the land masses were inverted mountains that scaled downwards from a flat wide mass to jagged peaks that ultimately narrowed to a stem planted into whatever was far below.

The sky was a stark contrast from that of the Dark

Realm. Hues of orange, and reds filled one side of the expanse, whilst the other was made up of lateral shades of blues, from light to dark. There were no moons or suns visible, yet light emanated from the reddish side giving the realm a surreal glow.

Their Yorian guides rode six-legged creatures that were much larger than their own huge mounts. The creatures were obviously bred for war, with oversized fangs and a horn protruding from between their eyes. The beasts' muscular bodies were covered in thick black hide from the neck down to their legs. A gray hide enveloped the heads.

Attacks on the Yorians' realm would prove very difficult as the only way to infiltrate would be crossing the bridge structures. Although an impressive array of spans, the Yorians could easily destroy them, making it impossible to reach them.

Following the Yori guides, they headed toward a large land mass in the center of the realm. Upon it, a castle with high turrets that jutted to dizzying heights stood proud. Much like their own ruler's castle, Indros' home was built to impress and intimidate. Joc looked over his shoulder at Kel, whose expression reflected his thoughts. There was no going back, the plan to remove the Dark Realm's current unworthy ruler was about to be set in motion.

Upon arriving at the castle, they were greeted by the sight of hundreds of Yorian warriors, both mounted and on foot.

Joc took in the sight calculating that their armies were about equal. The thoughts quickly vanished upon noting that, on two other land masses, just as many warriors stood watch. If the Torants went to war against the Yorians, there was little doubt the Yori would win. Why, then, had Indros not attacked their realm? And, more importantly, would the Yorian ruler keep his word allowing Joc and Kel to share rulership of the Dark Realm?

After they dismounted, Kel waited for Joc to near and spoke in a soft tone. "We must convince Gunther to conjure double the warriors, if we are to stand a chance against them."

"Yes, we must ensure to keep them from overtaking our realm," Joc replied.

Just then, Indros emerged and stood at the entrance, not moving forward, expecting them to address him as he stood atop a flight of stairs asserting his position of power.

Together the generals fell to one knee bending their heads. That done, they ascended the stairs to begin the meeting that had been arranged during Indros' visit.

Joc slid a look to Kel. One step at a time. First they would overthrow Gunther. He would ensure to deliver the killing blow so that the powers would be his. Then, he would dispense with Kel and become the ruler of the Dark Realm. It would take careful and deliberate plans, but it was all falling into place.

His ultimate plan was to become ruler over the Yorian Realm as well. It was much more desirable than the Dark Realm.

"WELCOME TO YORIAN," Indros said upon them entering the throne room. With towering ceilings and ornately decorated walls, the space exuded wealth. The throne consisted of a high-back chair with a set of chrome wings that extended wide and high. When the ruler sat upon the seat, it would look as if he bore wings.

Joc studied the mural behind it, which consisted of a battle scene. *Interesting.*

Indros wore intricately embroidered burgundy robes over loose fitting leg covers of the same color. He went to the throne and lowered himself upon it.

"Please sit," Indros motioned Joc and Kel to a pair of chairs that had been set facing the throne behind a table that was covered with platters of food and pitchers of drink.

Without waiting for them to finished settling, Indros motioned to the female. "This is my wife Sundi." Sitting on the left side of the throne was a beautiful female. She had flawless dark brown skin, amber eyes and long black silken tresses that were wrapped in golden threads. The female, dressed in flowing soft robing, studied them without expression.

The ruler motioned to a male on his right who remained standing in front of his chair. "He is my brother Rondo." The male was dressed similarly to Indros, only his clothes were not embroidered. He stood in front of his seat, arms crossed. He had the same coloring as Indros and Sundi, except his eyes were gray.

The brother's eyes narrowed. He turned to look at Indros. "Why are we hosting Torants?"

"Because we have a mutual interest at the moment," Indros replied patiently. "Sit, brother, so we can commence with discussions."

Rondo looked each of the generals in the eyes. It was not

hard to read what he thought in regard to their presence. The male would gladly spear them without a second thought.

Sundi rang a bell and immediately three pairs of servants rushed over holding trays, which they held in front of the trio. Indros plucked something from his tray and ate it. Only then did the two flanking him begin to eat and drink. The servants remained still, allowing them to eat from the trays they held.

A second set of servants brought food and placed it on the table in front of the generals. By the looks of disgust, even the servants did not care for their presence.

As it would be insulting not to eat, Joc and Kel ate from the offerings, which were not the Torant's usual fare that consisted mainly of meat and root bulbs. The fare before them was elaborately constructed from greens and brightly colored floral dishes. The only meat was sliced so thinly, it was hard to identify.

As was their custom, Joc and Kel ignoring the eating utensils and ate with their hands, not caring about the curious study of the Yorian rulers and others who stood around the room.

"I can easily guess why you came seeking my counsel. What I do not understand is why you would feel compelled to," Indros stated.

Joc swallowed the food in his mouth, wiping it with the back of his hand. "You proposed a joining of the realms upon your visit to our ruler. With that in mind, we come to offer something along the lines of an alliance if you assist us in trouncing the unworthy male who sits upon our throne."

"What type of assistance?" Rondo asked. "Why would

we help you?" Something akin to disgust dripped from the statement.

Kel huffed. "We are here as a result of your brother's visit. Gunther has no plans for any kind of a pact between our realms." He turned his attention to Indros. "Is part of your plan to eventually overtake both realms?"

The direct question seemed to take Indros by surprise as he hesitated, a goblet halfway to his mouth. He gave a one shouldered shrug, drank from the cup and placed it back on the tray. "The thought has crossed my mind. Although I must admit noticing how very dreary and dank the realm is. I am not sure there is anything to gain from the Dark Realm."

But on the land beyond there was much to gain. The lighter realms beyond were rich with minerals, jewels and lush lands. It was those realms that Indros sought to take over. Other than to add Torants into his army, the Dark Realm would provide the bridge between the Yorian and the more desirable realms.

The thought of Indros taking over the army made Joc hesitate. If he was to do this right, he would have to ensure to keep power over the Dark Realm and the forces within. Killing Gunther would mean the dominant dark powers would fill him and, with that, he could easily defend the realm. The darkness was powerful and stronger than any other magic in the lands. What an idiot Gunther was not to allow it free rein. And yet, it was that reluctance that would be his downfall and prove fortunate for Joc.

Indros waved the servants with trays away. "Send in the scribe," he said to a nearby guard. "Where is she by the way?"

The guard looked to Sundi, who shrugged. "She died."

Indros laughed and spoke to the generals. "My wife is quite possessive. I do have to spend long private times with a scribe." He turned to Sundi. "I will indulge you this once, but no more. Having a scribe for a longer period ensures proper records are kept. As it is, no one wishes for the post. Whether male or female, you have found ways to...er remove them."

Sundi didn't seem at all bothered by the chastisement, instead, she looked toward the entrance as an older male was ushered in.

The male didn't seem intimidated. He walked directly to the throne, bowed first to Indros, then secondly to Sundi. "I am called Basdin, your highness," he stated in a clear voice.

Sundi's smile reached her eyes. "Basdin! I have not seen you in years. How clever they are to appoint you as scribe." She clapped and beamed at Indros. "Basdin is my cousin and childhood confidant."

Basdin looked much older than Sundi, so Joc surmised the female had used magic to retain her youthful appearance.

The new scribe went to stand at a chair behind a small table and waited to be instructed to sit.

Indros indicated for the male to sit and then turned his attention back to the generals. "The Torants are here on behalf of the Dark Realm. They request our assistance in overthrowing their ruler and becoming the rulers themselves." Indros hesitated, studying both Joc and Kel.

"Although I suspect one will kill the other to gain ultimate control."

Joc's heart hammered in his chest. Of course, why had he not guarded his thoughts? Indros could read minds. Instead of reacting he shook his head as if thinking the claim ridiculous and looked to Kel. "Do you plan to kill me then?"

At Kel's flat gaze, he wasn't sure what to think. Instead, he spoke to Indros. "There is no reason why Kel and I cannot share overseeing the Dark Realm. Of course, whomever delivers the killing blow will absorb Gunther's powers. But then the other will assume the role of chief council. Absolute power over the army."

"As you say," Indros replied and returned his attention to the scribe. "Add General Joc's comments to the scroll."

The ruler rose from the throne, his robes flowing behind him as he paced across the room like a wolf circling prey. "Let's hear it. I have my own designs, but I'm curious what sort of treachery you'd suggest first."

"We need you as a distraction," came Joc's cold reply. "Gunther still expects your return. His attention, and his power, will be fixed on you and your guards. That gives one of us the perfect opportunity to strike. Once he's dead, we honor the agreement of a safe passage through the Dark Realm to wherever it is you truly want to go. But not our realm, that will remain ours."

Indros gave a slow, deliberate shake of his head, the barest hint of a sneer curling his lip. "We have no interest in your cursed realm. It's Esland we want. The nether border has proven...inconvenient. You lot can keep your shadows and rotting soil."

Kel narrowed his eyes, heat sparking behind them. The insult wasn't subtle. "No one breaks through Esland's defenses. Not even with your large number of warriors, and certainly not with your lumbering beasts."

A flicker of amusement crossed Indros' face. "Yes, yes. The mighty dragons of Esland. Breathing fire and noble nonsense. Spare me your opinions. I only need a crack in the wall; something your realm's endless mists have thus far denied me."

Joc leaned forward, his voice low and hard. "Even if we permit you through our borders, the mists bordering Esland devour anyone who enters. Magic fails. Men vanish. You wouldn't last a suns rise."

Indros waved a hand dismissively, as if already bored with the discussion. "There's another way. A less...sanctioned path, which cuts through a sliver of the Sisters' realm. But that's my concern, not yours," he said referring to Atlandia.

He met both Kel and Joc's eyes head-on, his voice laced with mockery. "Just play your part, generals. Be a martyr, or a victor, whichever suits you best. I don't care, as long as Gunther dies."

Prince Stirling's sisters Esmeralda and Rubiana ruled over the largest realm, Atlandia, an area that was as beautiful as it was deadly. During the cold season, a storm called 'the icing' struck daily across most of it. Only wolf sentinels and shifters native to the realm could survive the onslaught of the cutting ice that fell from the skies and the frigid temperatures.

Both Joc and Kel expected that Indros was not interested in their realm because of the icing, Yorian warriors could not survive it.

In a way, Atlandia could be considered a wasteland, if not for the fact that every day the land thrived, as the icing did not kill native flora or animals.

To Torants, the Dark Realm was filled with treasures of magic, of creatures and landscapes that existed nowhere else. It was the homeland of their species and although not beautiful it was where all Torants were born and hoped to die.

"I will visit at the passing of the allotted time. Whether your plan is successful or not is to be seen." Indros walked toward a set of windows, his back to them.

Joc and Kel stood, at the signaling the meeting had come to an end.

CHAPTER TWELVE

Aubrey stood just inside the yoga studio, the subtle scent of fresh paint mingling with lavender and citrus from the sachets she'd carefully tucked into a display basket. She faced the reception area, taking in the space with a contented sigh. On one end of the sleek wooden counter, a glowing salt lamp bathed the surface in a warm amber hue. On the other, a delicate flower arrangement of orchids and eucalyptus brought a touch of elegance and life. Centered on the counter a flat-screen tablet gleamed, ready for clients to book classes, schedule treatments, or sign up for memberships with a simple tap.

She turned to admire the cozy nook to the right. Two plush chairs, upholstered in calming shades of sage and ivory, framed a small table stacked with neatly arranged handouts. Business cards fanned out beside sachets tied with twine, their scent crisp and inviting. That bright burst of lavender and citrus seemed to breathe energy into the air.

Soft, ambient music of flutes and trickling water played

from hidden speakers, weaving a tranquil feel to the space. Across the front windows stood a long table, soon to be draped with linens and adorned with a vibrant spread of finger foods. Just inside the entrance, space had been cleared for a small bar wine, herbal teas, perhaps a celebratory cocktail or two.

In just a couple of hours, guests would arrive for the grand opening. And judging by the steady stream of RSVP messages and social media buzz, it was going to be more than just well-attended. It would be a celebration of her new beginning.

Erin burst through the door holding a huge bouquet of flowers. Behind her, Padriag entered carrying bags overflowing with small decorative boxes.

"I finished them!" Erin announced as she took one of the boxes from the bags. "See-through window so they can see the chocolate." She held it up proudly, adorned with a tiny bouquet that had to have taken forever to put together. "I made fifty."

Aubrey's mouth fell open. "You must have spent the entire day on it. They are absolutely lovely." Indeed they were, the guests would be delighted with them.

Her cousin shrugged. "Mum and Leti covered the classes today while I worked on them. It went rather smoothly."

"Can I put them down somewhere," Padriag asked lifting the bags and pretending they were too heavy.

"The three-tiered stand on the side table will hold them nicely." Aubrey took one of the bags showing Padriag where to put the other one.

Erin shooed her away. "I am sure you have plenty to do, Padriag and I will work on this display."

Two hours later, dressed in a breezy floral dress and strappy sandals, Aubrey stood by the entrance of BreYea Yoga, welcoming guests, giddy with nerves and excitement.

The studio buzzed with laughter and conversation, the energy vibrant and affirming. Just as she'd hoped, the turnout was fantastic, especially after Gwen and Tammie arrived bringing along a group of friends from Culross.

Liam, one of the men who'd escaped the other realm, arrived with his partner John, who often attended classes at the Edinburgh studio. The couple was handsome, dressed in what looked to be perfectly tailored slacks, John in a polo shirt and Liam in a fitted long-sleeve shirt. No polos for Liam, not yet anyway. Aubrey suspected the Brit would soften as he spent more time in the casual surroundings of Scotland.

"It's beautiful," Gwen breathed, turning in a slow circle to take in the softly lit studio. "So serene. Peaceful, even with all these people here."

Aubrey's heart swelled at the praise, her fingers absently brushing the edge of a nearby table. "That's exactly what I hoped for," she said, her voice warm. "A sanctuary. A little haven from the chaos."

"That's exactly what it feels like," came a familiar voice. John approached, holding a glass of wine in one hand. "And you, my friend, look stunning tonight." He leaned in to kiss her cheek just as her gaze shifted toward the front door.

She froze.

Marcus stood just inside the threshold with a bouquet of flowers, a self-assured stance and soft curve to his lips.

"Oh, no."

Gwen and John instinctively followed her line of sight.

"Who's that?" Gwen asked, her eyes moving back and forth.

"My ex," Aubrey said tightly. "Marcus. Believe it or not, he owns the space two doors down."

"Ah," Gwen said carefully. "So...not a welcome surprise?"

"Not even a little," Aubrey muttered, just as Marcus began weaving his way through the crowd toward them. John moved as if to intercept him, but Aubrey caught his arm.

"Let me," she whispered.

"Marcus," she said when he reached them, keeping her tone neutral. "I didn't expect to see you here."

His eyes flicked briefly to where her hand rested on John's arm, but his smile didn't budge. That was Marcus, always polished, always unreadable. Too smooth for his own good.

"I wouldn't miss the chance to wish you luck," he said, offering her the bouquet. "Best of luck with your little endeavor."

There it was. That subtle condescension wrapped in charm that she'd ignored while they were dating. How had she stayed with him for so long?

The statement made her blood boil; heat rose to her face. Of course he would make a condescending comment. But she hoped to keep her composure. Before she could speak, John spoke up.

"Expanding an enterprise is never a small feat. As a business owner myself, I am quite proud of Aubrey's courage to open a second storefront. Given the success of the first, all her friends expect this studio to be a triumph."

Marcus' mask fell. He'd expected the Aubrey he'd dated to give her usual response, explaining how she'd work hard and hope for the best.

But she didn't feel intimidated. Instead, she was surer than ever of her upcoming venture. She released John's hand and smiled broadly at Marcus. "If membership continues to grow as it has begun, I may need to buy you out soon." She laughed as if it was a joke, but in truth, it wasn't a bad plan to expand for additional classes at the same class time.

"What is your business?" John asked as Liam came to stand next to him.

He dug a card from his coat pocket and passed it to John. "Archer Physical Therapy. It is much needed here."

"Hmm," Liam said, studying the card John held. "There is already a therapy clinic near here. Are you aware? It may be a struggle to take patients away from an existing trusted practice."

"We shall see," Marcus replied curtly and then turned his attention to Aubrey, ignoring the men.

Whether he was aware of the other practice or not, Marcus didn't bother with a reply. Instead, he met Aubrey's gaze. The flowers brushed her hands as her ex held them out. "These are for you." He smiled in the way he always did after upsetting her. It had perhaps worked in the past, but not now.

Aubrey took the flowers while wondering why, when they dated, she'd not noticed how Marcus had found it easy to dish out criticism but rarely took it well. Then realization struck that he belittled others to make himself feel better.

Thankfully Marcus didn't linger around her for long. When Zina and Jeffrey arrived, he went to chat with them.

The evening was a success, and by the time it ended, the membership was much higher than she'd hoped for.

Apparently, the woman who'd taught yoga at the local community center had just retired, and those not wishing to exercise in the park were glad for the comfort of an indoor studio. They had gladly jumped at the opportunity to join using the grand opening discount.

"That went well," Erin said, returning from putting the leftover wine and snacks into her car.

Aubrey turned in a circle, arms extended. "I am so incredibly happy and excited and nervous and...did I say happy?"

"Yes you did, but you are allowed to say it twice," Erin replied with a wide grin. "The studio will do great. I have little doubt."

"I open in a couple days. Still have to hire an additional instructor. Already have a receptionist."

Erin gave her a hug. "I will be here for the first week to help out with training. Just let me know the times."

"You are the best," Aubrey said meaning it. "Now scoot. I am going to lock up and head home."

THE NEXT DAY, taking advantage of the two days off, Aubrey made her way around the cellar. The air smelled damp despite a pair of slender windows being propped open.

John and Gwen had organized things and left her a note listing boxes they thought she should go through. So far they claimed to not have found anything of interest.

A lone bulb hung from the ceiling, reminding Aubrey of old scary movies. It seemed that in every basement or cellar scene where victims were locked in, a lone bulb hung from the ceiling. To dispel her imagination getting away from her, she played cheery music from her phone and switched on an old lamp Gwen or John had set up atop what looked to be an antique table.

The additional light and music made the space less scary as she opened a box and found figurines wrapped in bubble wrap. She needed to call her parents and make a case for taking most of the things in the cellar to a charity shop.

Sounds of steel drums and island sounds filled the space. Aubrey jumped to her feet, and began dancing, swaying her hips to the rhythm of the music and waving her hand over her head. "Jamin' Jamin' Jamin' to the music," she sang.

She turned in a full circle, pretending to be on a sandy beach in the Caribbean, the salty air in her hair and bright sun on her face.

"Jam—" when she went for a second turn, the realization that she wasn't alone stopped her mid-word and Aubrey let out a wild scream. She picked up the nearest item, a house figurine and hurled it at the man.

Upon hitting Gunther's chest, the figurine burst into shards that fell to the floor. He scowled down the pieces and then at her. "I thought you'd noticed I was here," he said, not moving.

Aubrey held a second figurine up, this one a horse. "Are

you possessed?" Both her voice and hand shook. How would she know if he'd turned evil?

"I am not sure what you mean?" Gunther's deep accented voice was sharp. "I am the same as before."

She took a step forward, the horse at the ready, and looked into his eyes. Admittedly, it was the wrong thing to do because visions of their kiss flooded her addled brain and her face heated.

"All right. I suppose you do look the same. I am not sure how I would be able to tell if you were consumed by evil."

His wide shoulders lifted and lowered. "I suppose you will sense it. I will not come near you if the darkness overtakes me." He looked around the space. "Is this where you hope to find something to help me?"

Aubrey put the horse down gently and lifted her phone to turn off the music. "Not to help you, but to see if there is something that is causing this." She motioned between them. "Since I don't know anything about magic or such, I have no idea what exactly to look for."

He was dressed casually this day, with brown slacks, a blue pullover and joggers. The blue shirt made his eyes seem especially brighter. The blue pools making it hard to tear her gaze away.

Forcing herself to look away, she motioned to a stack of small boxes. "I am going to sort through those today. If you wish, you can do it with me."

Why was she inviting an evil being to hang out? Aubrey prayed he'd say no.

"I was going to offer to help."

Suddenly awkward, Aubrey wasn't sure how to handle things. "Do you want something to drink?"

"Perhaps later." He moved to the first box, lifted it and placed it on a table. Then he motioned to it. "Do you wish me to open it?"

Aubrey nodded and then stood transfixed as he reached to his side and took a dagger from a sheath she'd not noticed. While he cut through the packing tape, head bent, it was as if he were a normal guy helping her. A very hot, but regular guy. Not one who ruled an entire realm, a king of sorts. A ruler who wielded magical powers and was equal parts good and evil.

"How does it feel?" Aubrey asked. "To have powers and rule an entire...realm?" She reached into the box and took out a pair of wrapped bundles.

A crease formed between Gunther's brows as he considered her question. "I am still not accustomed to it. It is as if currents of electric..." he pointed to the swaying lightbulb. "As if currents travel under my skin constantly. I do not care for it. However, when I have dark thoughts, when the darkness beckons, the sensations are different, enjoyable...I suppose you can call it stimulating."

He lifted a wrapped bundle and Aubrey nodded, giving him permission to tear it open. She did the same to the two she'd dug out. All three were part of a set, cups and saucers with matching floral motifs. The rest of the box was the same, all with the same pattern.

Gunther lifted the box and placed it next to the other items she planned to donate. "Two to go," Aubrey said.

Curiously, as they worked, opening boxes and going

through the items, she didn't want him to leave. He was good company, not pushing for a conversation and he'd not tried to do anything to make her feel uncomfortable. If anything, she was the one who couldn't tear her gaze away when their eyes met, and who stole glances at him when he busied himself opening boxes or digging through them.

"What do you think about this?" He held a tarnished pewter goblet. "It looks to be quiet old."

Aubrey walked closer, studying the object, timid to touch it. "Do you sense anything? I would think that you would know better than me."

"I am not sure that I would," Gunther admitted. "To be honest, like you, I have no idea what to look for or that, if we do find the item, I will know."

"Let me see," Aubrey held out her hand and he gave her the goblet. At their fingers touching, awareness spread up her arm. Begrudgingly, she admitted to herself that she could be holding the Holy Grail, and it was doubtful she'd realize it. A look or touch from Gunther was more powerful than the garish goblet. "I will put this aside. So far it's the only item we have found of interest."

They held each other's gazes for a beat too long. "We should talk," Aubrey began.

Gunther didn't break eye contact. "About the kiss?" His attention moved to her lips. "I think about it all the time."

Her breath caught. "Yes, well we shouldn't have. I was impulsive and being who you are, I prefer it not happen again."

Taking a step closer, his eyes narrowed. "I would prefer it to happen again and often. You are different from any woman I have ever known. What I mean is, had known, before I went to the other realm."

Unable to stop herself, Aubrey wondered if the women in his realm were more beautiful and if he'd been in any relationship there. "What are the women in the other realm like?"

Gunther dropped his gaze. "The females in the Dark Realm are from a race called Torant. They are large, tall as me, humanlike, but have elongated faces, like a horse...or maybe a wolf."

"That doesn't sound attractive," Aubrey said. "Are there no humans there?"

"In the other realm where I lived for many years, there are women who live in the villages."

As she was about to ask how long it had been since he'd been with a woman, dongs of bells sounded. Someone was at the front door.

"Keep looking. I will be right back." Aubrey hurried up the stairs. The interruption was a good thing. Asking about other women would give Gunther the wrong impression. That she was interested in him.

Catching her reflection in a hallway mirror, she hesitated. Cheeks flushed, eyes bright, she looked excited, happy even. Her hormones were definitely working.

Without looking, she opened the door prepared to sign for a package. Instead, Marcus stood there, his hand up as if to knock.

"Aubrey." He gave her a crooked smile. "Can we talk?"

It took several seconds for the fact that her ex stood at the door to sink in. The hesitation gave Marcus the impression he could enter, and he walked past her to stand in the front parlor.

"I'd forgotten how grand this house is," Marcus said looking around the space. "It has always taken my breath. This was to be our home. Remember?"

The ability to speak finally happened and Aubrey took a breath. "What do you want Marcus? I thought I made it clear that I am not interested. You and I will not get back together."

Looking her in the eyes, Marcus took a step toward her, and she took one back. "Aubrey, honestly. Everyone makes mistakes, and you of all people should understand. After all, wasn't I a mistake? You were dating someone else when we met."

"How dare you!" She couldn't keep her tone even. "Unlike you, I was honest with Andrew and broke things off before agreeing to go out with you. You cheated on me. I have moved past it."

There was a gleam of triumph in his expression. "So, you have forgiven me then?"

"Please leave and don't return."

"Aubrey..."

"She said leave." Gunther walked into the room and came to stand next to Aubrey. His sheer size made the slender, five-foot-ten Marcus look like an adolescent by comparison.

Marcus' mouth opened, but he recovered quickly, his eyes narrowing at Aubrey. "Does he know about us?"

To his credit, Gunther allowed her to speak, not doing

more than standing by silently. At the same time, she could sense the irritation emanating from him.

"There is no us. There hasn't been for over a year." Aubrey looked up at Gunther. "Gunther, this is Marcus. He was my partner until he cheated on me."

Gunther's eyebrows shot up. "Then he is a fool."

By the flare of his nostrils and lips pressed into a tight line, Marcus was furious. He was not so much of an idiot to challenge Gunther. "Is he your lover?"

Aubrey rolled her eyes. "Go home Marcus. Leave Linlithgow. There is no reason for you to be here."

When Marcus hesitated, Gunther took a step forward and Marcus' eyes widened. Not only was Gunther huge, but the jagged scar that ran down the side of his face made him look like a ruthless killer. With one hand, he grabbed the front of Marcus' shirt lifting him from the ground effortlessly.

"Leave and do not bother her again." He walked to the still-open front door and shoved Marcus out. Then he closed the door firmly. Keeping his back to her, Gunther let out a long breath.

When he turned, Aubrey lost her ability to breathe at the sight of a wide smile and dimples.

"I kept it at bay," Gunther said, still grinning. "The darkness. It was not hard. I was able to do so easily."

Aubrey couldn't help it; she smiled back and allowed him to wrap his arms around her. Hugging her tightly, he spoke into her ear. "I will always protect you."

Her entire body came to life at the feel of his against hers. If only they could remain like this, not breaking apart. She inhaled his scent, felt the softness of his hair against her cheek. The strength of his arms, enveloping her and the hard expanse of his chest. Being held by him was the most protected she'd ever felt. Even her father did not give her the safe harbor of Gunther's embrace.

Recalling her promise to Erin and the others, she pushed away. "I have to head back downstairs and go through the last box."

Gunther nodded at the implication she didn't want him to go with her. "My presence is not welcome."

She closed her eyes and tilted her head back. "I am torn between who you are and what you represent. I am attracted to you. If you were from here, we would probably be in my bed by now. But I promised the others, and so did you, that we would stay away from each other. And yet here we are."

"I cannot stop thinking about you. Please do not send me away." When he closed the distance between them and claimed her mouth, she was lost.

When she took his hand and pulled him to her bedroom, Audrey refused to think, to consider this could be the biggest mistake of her life. All she knew was that this man had claimed her entirely since the first time they'd met. He was to be hers, and consequences be damned. For the last months, she'd devoted her time and energy to the studio, to her friends and to this house. She'd always been the last priority. This time, she would not deny herself.

Once in her bedroom, she closed the door and turned to him.

Clashing against each other with unspoken knowledge that their time was limited, they kissed and tore at their clothing, removing and tossing the items aside. Some landed on furniture or the floor.

Fully nude, Gunther stood before her; utterly, devastatingly real. His body was beautiful, powerful, but it wasn't perfection that stole her breath, it was the story etched into his skin. Faint silver lines crisscrossed his chest, brutal reminders of horrors survived. A rough, uneven scar near his lower abdomen spoke of pain endured without mercy or proper care. And when her gaze met his, her eyes drifted to the jagged scar that ran along the side of his face, a wound that should have dulled his looks, but nothing could distract from his attractiveness.

He stepped closer, the heat from his body enveloping her before his arms did. With effortless strength, he lifted her, holding her as if she were something precious.

"You are the most beautiful thing I've seen in lifetimes," he murmured, his voice a low, reverent hum against her ear. "After so much darkness...to look at you feels like a sin, I'm not worthy of you."

He laid her down with a care that contradicted his size, his body following hers onto the bed.

"Are you sure?" he asked, his voice roughened by hope and restraint, eyes searching hers with uncertainty.

Aubrey didn't speak. Instead, she pressed her lips to his chest, where his heart beat steady and strong beneath her touch. Her kisses wandered slowly across the canvas of him, each mark, each scar. Her hand traced down his side, softly skimming over hard muscle, teasing, exploring, igniting. Her body responded to the feel of him, to the desire coiling between them.

Undeniable, unstoppable.

And still, he watched her as if she were the miracle he never thought he'd find.

He was already aroused, his member jutting proudly from between his legs. Aubrey waited, acknowledging it had probably been a long time since he'd been with a woman.

"I want this very much," she whispered against his ear. "When you get to know me, you will learn, I am strong-willed and fight for what I want. Right now, I really want you."

A soft moan escaped his parted lips, and he pulled her against him, his mouth once again claiming hers. Aubrey threw her leg over him, offering her body to him, needing to be taken fully.

When Gunther grasped her hip, she noted his hand trembled. His breathing was shallow, and he swallowed once, and then again.

Of course he was nervous.

Aubrey covered his hand with hers, waiting until he met her gaze. The uncertainty in his eyes melted her heart. She smiled at him. "I want to be with you Gunther, but if you are not ready, I completely understand."

"It has been a very long time since I've been with a woman..." He stopped speaking and kissed her lightly. "I am ready, perhaps much too ready."

Understanding dawned, he hoped he'd not finish too quickly and not satisfy her or something along those lines. "I only expect to be like this, touching, feeling your body against mine. Nothing more."

He gripped her hip tighter and with his other hand

guided himself, searching until prodding at her entrance. His eyes met hers for just a moment before he plunged.

With precise and energetic movements, they soon found the perfect rhythm. Gunther nuzzled into her hair, his body thrusting forward, pulling back and delving again deeper, harder.

Aubrey clung to his midback, her nails digging into his skin, her head thrown back. She'd made love before, but this was different, it was as if their bodies recognized the other and had come together after a long separation. She'd never be able to describe how consumed she was in that moment. The myriads of sensations colliding, overwhelming. In that moment Gunther was the only other person in her world. The feel of his body, the sounds he made from deep in his throat, the touch of his lips on her skin. It was like nothing she'd ever experienced before.

As cresting threatened, she found his mouth and took it, needing to be fully consumed.

The climax hit with so much strength, Aubrey let out a scream. Her entire body shuddered, her sex tightening around his.

In the haze of release, Gunther's hoarse moans echoed in her ear. The sound so sensual, a second pulse exploded in her.

"Ahhh!" Audrey raked her fingers down his back, stopping at his hips and holding him still. "Don't y-you dare m-move," she breathlessly demanded.

For his part, Gunther collapsed over her.

It was a long moment later that he stirred, pulled out and held himself up so not to crush her. He studied her face and slid a finger between her breasts, stopping on her stomach. "The color of your skin is rare. A creamy brown satin."

"We are definitely a contrast," Aubrey said holding her hand over his much lighter one. "You are the color of rich cream, but not pale."

He studied their hands, then took hers and lifted it to his lips. He pressed a kiss to her palm and met her gaze. "I do not know how to feel. You have given me a gift that I will always treasure."

Aubrey could feel her cheeks redden. "It was amazing," she finally replied. "You are very good in bed. You're very attractive and your body is amazing."

A frown crossed his features. "My face and body are nothing close to perfect."

Cupping his face, she kissed him. "I can't imagine what all you've been through but believe me when I tell you. You are very handsome. You're the hottest guy ever. And when not consumed by evil, you seem decent enough."

"Hot?" Confusion crossed his features. "What does hottest mean?"

She'd forgotten he lived in another realm. For some reason, the thought that she'd just had sex with a guy who ruled in another world seemed comical.

Aubrey giggled. "It means very attractive."

A smile played on the corners of his lips. "You are hot too."

Again, she giggled and caught sight of the time. "I hate to say this, but we need to get up and dressed. Erin and Padriag will be home soon."

They dressed in silence, sliding glances at one another in

a way a couple does when they have moved to another level in a relationship. Except they were not in a relationship. The sex was totally a one-time thing.

She was enthralled watching him pull the shirt on and button it, the garment fitting perfectly over the muscular arms and across broad shoulders. Even clothed, she wanted to touch him.

"Will you continue to search?" he asked. "I can return and help."

Aubrey raked her fingers through her curls, finding that, as expected, they'd exploded into a wild bush. "I will continue the search. I only have a couple boxes left to look through and then I'll search my grandmother's chests. If I find something, I will take it to the others."

"I only ask that you use it wisely. I don't know what whatever you find can do, be careful."

Pulling her into an embrace, he held her tightly and they kissed once more, so passionately, her knees almost gave out.

His breathing was ragged when he broke the kiss and met her gaze. "Until I see you again."

Then he was gone.

CHAPTER THIRTEEN

There was treachery thick in the air—Gunther could feel it coiling like a venomous snake around him. Let the generals play their petty games. Did they truly believe he wouldn't sense their betrayal? That he, the most powerful being across all realms, would fall to something as crude as a blade in the back?

Fools.

He'd read Meliot's tomes cover to cover, each one a chilling foretelling of deception and blood. He'd expected this. The Torants were nothing if not predictable, faithless creatures with no concept of honor. In their world, a knife sunk in while a back was turned was as natural as breathing.

But they'd made one fatal mistake: thinking Gunther could be taken down like any other man.

"Kill them. Butcher their bodies. Do it while our warriors watch," the Darkness demanded, a delectable fury simmering just under the surface of his foremost thoughts. *"The strength of the darkness is yours."*

"Gunther, as you can see, it is urgent that more warriors be conjured immediately," Kel stated, his eye looking somewhere past Gunther's left shoulder. "The threats on our western border grow with each passing day. Our current guard force is growing tired."

Whether the threat was real or not, Gunther doubted the situation was as dire as the generals were portraying it to be.

"I will go myself. It is not that I do not wish to conjure more warriors, it is that I am not sure of the proper process to ensure they are loyal only to me."

Joc straightened, his eyes filled with fury. "They should be loyal and obedient to not only you, Master, but also your leaders. Kel and I, your generals. Otherwise, how can we command the forces?"

"I stand corrected," Gunther acquiesced in a flat tone. "As I said. It will require days of research. For the time being, I can fortify the border magically. No one will be able to pass."

Joc held both hands up, as if stopping someone from approaching. "There is no need for magical intervention."

Gunther met the general's gaze and attempted to read his thoughts, but the Torant's mind was impenetrable. Someone with strong magic had placed wards on both of the general's minds.

He continued, ensuring to keep his expression blank. "Did you not just say the guard force is growing tired?"

"We did Master," Kel said. "However, if you install magical barriers, it will be seen as an insult to your warriors. A strong message that you do not trust them."

I don't. Gunther thought to himself.

If he were to be honest, there was not one being in the realm he trusted fully. The only person within the realms that he considered to be honest was Prince Sterling, but the prince could not help him here, he would never ever interfere in another kingdom's dealings.

Did Joc and Kel have plans that extended past their realm?

The Dark Realm, Atlandia and Esland, were sworn enemy territories. Over the decades they'd warred many times. Meliot, Gunther's predecessor, had never given up on the idea of overtaking the forbidden land, which was rumored to be breathtakingly beautiful.

However, what made Esland enticing was the existence of dragons there. Meliot had wanted to trap Prince Sterling who had control of the majestic beasts so that, in turn, he would use them against other realms and become the supreme ruler.

Fortunately, it was because of the dragons that no other realm had ever succeeded in infiltrating Esland and in all probability never would.

The relationship between the rulers of Atlandia and the Dark Realm was a more complicated one. There were scrimmages between the fighters, usually wolves against dark sentinels that resembled wolves, but it rarely escalated into a true battle. The magical protections of that realm kept intruders from going past the forest surrounding it. The wards were impenetrable and had held for centuries. Yet, on occasion, defectors from the Dark Realm had managed to get past the barrier. It was almost as if it were a living essence that understood the difference between enemy and ally.

One of the generals gave an impatient huff.

"What will you do to help your warriors? Do you plan to allow them to perish if there is an attack?" Joc demanded.

Gunther understood that it was only a matter of time when he would be able to continue in the role of ruler without using the dark powers to keep control. The warriors were bloodthirsty and were growing impatient. They thrived on war and destruction and any ruler who did not, had to be overthrown.

The darkness within him rose, overwhelming his senses.

"Conjure more warriors. Attack. War. You must. Release us. Just this once."

His body hummed with expectation. A sensation tempting him forward made him close his eyes.

Why not? On some level he thirsted for the satisfaction of allowing his powers free rein. To feel the full strength of what hummed within him.

"Very well. I will do it. You'll have your wish—more fighters." The words were his, yet not. His voice echoed strangely, layered, as though a chorus of Gunther's spoke at once, each with a different edge of power.

His legs moved of their own accord, carrying him from the throne room. Every nerve in his body sang with electricity, his fingertips tingling as raw energy surged beneath his skin, lightning caged in flesh.

"Taste it—our power, exquisite and unending. We are legions. We are everything." The voices slithered around him, hissing in a malevolent chorus. Could the others hear them? Or was madness wrapping its claws around his mind?

Gunther's thoughts spun, with warning bells and fear. *This isn't right. This will not end well.*

He tried to stop, to think, to resist. But his body ignored him. It was like an empty vessel now, marching forward as if pulled by invisible chains.

The loss of control was more than unsettling, it was horrifying. Yet even as he struggled, the dam inside him burst. The power he'd barely restrained came rushing in, a storm of dark magic, crashing over him in waves of rapture. The rush was so intense, so euphoric, his body shuddered from the force of it.

He reached the balcony.

With a cry that was more beast than man, Gunther threw his arms skyward. Blazing streaks of multicolored light, crimson, amber, gold shot from his fingers, making arcs across the night sky. Circles spun and collided, long cords of energy whipped and danced like cosmic fire.

From deep within, a guttural growl erupted, shaking the air. He lifted his arms again, this time unleashing a torrent so bright the reflection painted the courtyard in violent color.

Below, the Torant warriors had already gathered. Beasts, centaurs, and conjured warriors alike. They stood in awe, weapons raised as the darkness circled them with unholy hunger.

Then, as one, the chanting began.

"Hail our Ruler. Hail the darkness."

Over and over, a thunderous chant that shook the stones beneath them. Boots stomped like war drums, the rhythm feverish, unstoppable.

And at the heart of it all, Gunther stood, no longer merely a man.

He was the storm.

He was the weapon.

"It is time. Release more. Allow the power to consume you." Inside his head, the darkness' voices sounded louder than the chanting.

He formed the word "no" in his mind, but his lips did not obey. "Yes."

At the response, his body exploded into fragments of power, each part sending pulses of bliss through him.

Letting out a primal yell, he waved his hands over the warriors.

Screams sounded as one by one, the conjured fell to the ground and began convulsing, each body splitting in half, puddles of blood pooling under them. Dark pools of blood, soon covering most of the ground.

The two halves of each conjured writhed, wiggling like snakes. Then the halves split once again and then again. The conjured became six grotesque writhing pieces of flesh.

In a matter of moments, the creatures began transforming, first a head sprouting, then arms and finally legs. Within minutes, the creations struggled to stand, quivering as their bodies thickened, becoming muscular, human-like warriors, each one identical in features. Dark hair, a prominent square jaw, prominent brow, and thick necks.

Eventually rows and rows of conjured stood naked, their bodies pale in contrast to the dark surroundings, bare feet reddened by the spilled blood. The conjured were created to fight, powerfully built, their facial features twisted into the scowls of killers. They were the perfect weapons, impervious to the cold, strong and powerful and more importantly, without conscience or emotions.

Deep guttural barks of laughter overtook Gunther, his body completely taken over by a sensation he'd never known, the taste so sublime, he already craved more.

When he turned, the generals did their best to hide their expressions of satisfaction. Gunther chuckled, looking at them each in turn.

"If anyone is going to conquer another realm, it will be me. At dawn, I will declare war on the Yorian Realm."

The darkness within reveled. "*Yes. War. Yes. Death.*"

Finally, he understood the appeal of evil. Nothing could match the dizzying satisfaction of allowing it free rein.

Nothing could compare to the beauty of the darkness within him.

Gunther snapped his fingers, and both generals toppled over and began clawing at their necks, fighting against an invisible vise that squeezed.

The fools, the more they fought, the tighter the hold would become.

Stepping over the struggling Torants, he took a few steps before snapping his fingers again, satisfied at the sound of them gulping in air.

He looked over his shoulder at the Torants, who were too weak to stand. "Do you really think you can kill me?"

Neither responded, they were too busy coughing and sputtering.

"*There is much to do,*" the darkness hissed. "*Together we will conquer realms*"

His lips curved. But it wasn't him, Gunther realized. He was being overshadowed by the many who were the darkness.

"We will go to war against the Yorians, yes, but there is another realm that is more exciting. The human realm. You have gained access; it is time for us to test our powers there."

"No." Gunther pushed both hands against his temples. "I will not."

"We can, and we will," the darkness said. *"We have been waiting for our powers to be this strong so that we can finally conquer the ultimate realm. We will be the most powerful ruler to exist."*

"I will not." Gunther fought against the dark thoughts with all his strength.

What had he done?

Allowing the darkness even a sliver of freedom had been a fatal mistake. Now it surged through him like poison in his veins, seizing control inch by inch. The thing inside him was no longer content to lurk in edges of his subconscious. Instead, it was becoming dominant. And soon...it would devour him completely.

Clenching his jaw, Gunther squeezed his eyes shut and fought back, pushing against the suffocating tide of malevolence with every shred of his will. For a fleeting second, he gained the upper hand, but the hold was paper-thin, fragile as glass. He could feel it cracking.

"Aubrey..." His voice was raw, strangled. "H-Help me..."

Something like a gut punch struck and he let out a gasp. He staggered, collapsing against the cold, stark throne, not to sit upon it, but to keep himself upright. He didn't want to rule. Especially not *this* place. Not the Dark Realm, where evil slithered through the air and shadows became his traitors.

This was a war he could never win alone. But alone he was, surrounded by creatures who thrived on death and destruction, haunted by the monster clawing its way out from within him.

His body convulsed, muscles trembling with the strain. Sweat slicked his brow. His vision blurred. The darkness wasn't just inside him—it was *everywhere*, seeping from the walls, curling across the floor like smoke, alive with hunger.

And then he broke.

Gunther let out a ragged moan as his legs gave out. He hit the floor hard, the impact jolting the breath from his lungs. Crawling with the last of his strength, he dragged himself behind a long, ancient sideboard hoping to hide from anyone coming in with plans to kill him.

Silence fell...but it wasn't peace. It was triumph.

The darkness coiled through the chamber, pulsing with malevolent glee. Misty tendrils slithered through the air, celebrating their release.

The human had been strong. But not strong enough.

And once set free...

Evil never returned to its cage.

CHAPTER FOURTEEN

"What's wrong?" Erin asked, a concerned look on her face. "You stopped talking midsentence."

Aubrey shook her head. "Did I? My mind wandered and for a moment, I thought I heard a voice."

Even in the dim light of the cellar, Aubrey felt as if it was too bright. As if she'd been in total darkness and stepped into light. She narrowed her eyes.

"What did you hear?" Erin asked. "You looked scared."

It was best to be honest. As long as she didn't tell Erin about the tryst with Gunther. That was a secret she'd never divulge.

"I heard Gunther's voice asking for help." She shook her head. "It was as if I was in another place. A dark, shadowed room filled with swirls of lights that brightened and dimmed."

"Oh no," Erin exclaimed putting down a figurine and

closing the distance between them. She took Aubrey by the shoulders. "Do you feel faint?"

Aubrey pushed her cousin's hands away. "I feel fine. Just shaken a bit. What if he's in danger?"

"It's probably a trick," Erin replied. "He is using you to try to get here. We can't let that happen. He is a dangerous man."

It was on the tip of her tongue to tell Erin she didn't believe it to be so. The connection she'd had with Gunther had been pure. But, if it proved to be something other than that, she'd feel like an utter fool.

For the moment, it was best not to say anything. The first thing that would happen is that Erin would call on Gwen, Tammie and John to do some sort of protection spell. It wasn't that she didn't want their help, if it were needed, but at the moment, she wanted to hear from Gunther. To know he was okay.

"One more box and then we'll consider the attic and the dusty trunks," Aubrey said with a shudder. "I want to get this over with today. After tomorrow, I'll be too busy at the studio to do anything."

She dug into the box, lifting a thick woolen fabric. Under it, there were three bubble wrapped items. She lifted a bundle, it was heavy, but impossible to tell what it was through the uneven covering. Carefully, Aubrey, pulled the tape off and unwrapped it.

"What is that?" Erin asked peering down at a phallic shaped metal piece. "Is it something sexual?"

Aubrey giggled. "I don't know, think it separates from the middle."

Not touching it directly, Aubrey used two tea towels from another box and pulled the cover apart. They let out gasps because inside was an intricately carved crystal dagger. About six inches long, the dagger's blade glistened in the dim light. Even to her inexperienced eye, it was obvious the blade was dangerously sharp. It was beautiful.

The handle was golden and encrusted with precious stones that Aubrey guessed to be rubies, emeralds and topaz.

"Whoa," Erin said in a reverent tone. "That has to be worth a lot of money."

Aubrey nodded. "I have no doubt the stones are real. She held it up on her palms. Look on the end of the handle, are those diamonds?"

Could this be it? Was this dagger what was needed to save Gunther? Aubrey met Erin's gaze and knew her cousin was thinking the same thing.

"We need to take it to the castle," Erin said. "Here give it to me."

The dagger became heavy in her hands and when she attempted to hand it to Erin, a sizzle of protest zapped up her arm. She gasped and pulled the dagger closer. Immediately it lightened, it was almost as if it sighed in relief.

"I don't think it wants me to give it to anyone. I know this is going to sound crazy, but I am sensing it cannot be taken out of the house."

"Oh." Erin looked around and grabbed a wooden lidded box. "Let's put it back in its sheath and into the box. I'll go and call the others to come here."

The blade seemed to glow when Aubrey glanced at it. Probably her imagination. "Good idea."

Taking her time, she returned the blade to its protective cover and then into the box. She let out a breath. "I am not sure how I feel about it being here in the house. It is definitely magical."

Erin nodded. "Since it hasn't caused any harm before, I doubt anything will change. Should we continue looking?" She motioned to the box.

"Yes."

They each took one of the two remaining bundles. Erin unwrapped another bundle and discovered a leather strap with a round gold pendant. Etched in the pendant was the bust of a human-looking creature. Broad shoulders, a thick neck and a face with an elongated nose and mouth resembling a dog, or perhaps a horse.

"Look at this," Erin said holding the strap, the pendant swinging from it.

"Eww," Aubrey said. "He's ugly." She peered into the box. "I'm afraid to open the last one."

She waited a beat while Erin wrapped the necklace up and then she lifted the third bundle. It was of a good weight, like that of a medium-sized rock. Trepidation surged inside her as she pulled back the tape, then the bubble wrap. The item was bound in an intricately embroidered fabric.

On the fabric, embroidered in a golden thread, there were depictions of strangely shaped trees, the bare branches intermingling to form a border around the edges.

Heart beating wildly, she pulled back the fabric to find a beautifully carved bowl. It was black, perhaps onyx, although it was hard to tell what exactly it was made of. It was the size of a soup bowl, not that anyone would use such a beautiful item for soup. Other than something like floral designs on the outer edge, she didn't sense anything from it.

"Are there any words on it?" Erin asked peering at the bowl.

Aubrey flipped it to look on the bottom, but it was smooth. She shrugged. "Nothing that I can see. Maybe it was just a keepsake."

Why were the pendant and the bowl stored under the cloth together? Nothing made sense. Aubrey had a sudden thought that sent shivers down her spine.

If the last dagger they'd found was the only weapon that could kill Meliot, was it possible, the blade they'd just found was the only item powerful enough to end Gunther's life?

If only she'd found it when he'd been there, he could have told her more. Now that Erin knew, her cousin wouldn't hesitate to inform the others of the find.

"I am not sure I want to do anything with this." She took the pendant and bowl and placed them in the same wooden box where the dagger was. "It may be best to leave these things here and not move them. We cannot chance the consequences of our friends coming and releasing something too strong to be controlled."

At least Erin seemed to be listening. Whether she'd changed her mind wasn't clear. "It could be a way to keep Gunther away from you. From the possibility of evil breaking through to this realm."

"What about that strange creature? What if that thing is what is trying to create an opening? I don't feel as if Gunther is being deceitful. I believe he wants to be freed and get away from the Darkness."

Erin's gaze met hers. "I know you must feel something for him. But the darkness is very powerful. Whether or not he fights, eventually it will win."

She let out a breath. "Padriag told me Meliot was not an evil man before being overtaken by the Darkness. The wizard himself told Padriag that it is impossible to fight against the overwhelmingly intoxicating force of evil."

"Can we give it until week's end? I really need to rest up for the opening tomorrow and that is what I want to concentrate on. I cannot allow all of this to interfere."

"I think it's a good idea. I will tell Padriag about it when he returns home. If he wishes to delve into things, do you mind?"

She wasn't thrilled at the idea. "It means the others will follow quickly. That's what I'm trying to avoid."

Finally her cousin let out a breath. "Fine, I won't tell him today, but I can't keep it from him for long. I don't like keeping secrets from him."

"Thank you," Aubrey hugged Erin and then took her upper arm guiding her to the staircase. "I need a glass of wine. You?"

"Great idea."

They walked from the cellar and Aubrey turned to pull the string on the light. Just as she touched it, a glimmer caught her attention.

The flaps of the box had opened and a sliver of what looked like glitter emanated from it. A second later, it vanished.

"What is it?" Erin asked at her hesitation.

"I almost lost my balance reaching for this damn string,"

Aubrey lied. After another quick glance at the box, she pulled the string.

IT WAS dark by the time Aubrey pulled up to the familiar circular driveway in front of her home, the following day. She was both exhausted and exuberant. Things couldn't have gone any more perfectly. Every class had been full, and she'd hired a new yoga instructor who'd led a faultless beginner's class under Aubrey's watchful eye.

The last class ended at six and she kept the studio open until seven at night, time she used to clean up and prepare for the next day.

The studio was open Tuesday through Thursday and half a day on Fridays. It was a good schedule, giving Aubrey time for other things. She'd learned from her mother not to overdo it and always allow for balance in her life.

Aubrey let out a sigh when seeing that besides Erin and Padriag's Land Rover, three additional cars were parked on the driveway.

She'd known her cousin wouldn't be able to keep from telling her husband about the items they'd found. If she were to be honest, it was what Erin should've done. Keeping secrets was not a good way to start a marriage.

She walked around her car, opened the door, and grabbed her work tote.

Her evening plans had been to search and comment on any online reviews for the studio and drink a glass of Cabernet. Instead, as she walked into the house, the aroma of delicious herbs and garlic as well as the sounds of conversations greeted her.

Oscar greeted her with his usual air of supremacy seeming to complain about the visitors he'd not approved of. "You, sir, will have your dinner in here." She ran her hand over the cat's back, stopping when Oscar sat and glared up at her. Apparently, her petting skills needed work.

She deposited her tote on a wingback chair and strolled into the kitchen. "Hello all. It smells delicious in here. Who cooked?"

"I did," Gwen lifted a hand with a fork in it. "We got hungry after..." She hesitated and glanced at Erin, who had the decency to look chagrined.

"After studying the three things we found yesterday." Aubrey gave Erin what she hoped was an understanding look. Erin visibly relaxed.

Also in the room were Sabrina Campbell, Gwen's sister, Tristan McRainey, Gwen's husband and Gavin Campbell, Sabrina's drop-dead gorgeous partner.

After opening a can of cat food and serving Oscar, she returned to the kitchen, her stomach rumbling in anticipation.

Aubrey plucked a plate from the two that were left on the edge of the kitchen island and began piling food onto it. "The only thing I ate today was a power bar. I am starving."

She climbed onto the only empty stool and gratefully accepted a glass of wine from Erin. "So, what have you discovered?" Aubrey took a bite of the herbed chicken and almost swooned. Spearing green beans, she waited for someone to say anything.

"We do not think they are anything more than decorations," Tristan said. "None of us picked up on there being any magic attached."

"It could be there is nothing in this house. Or at least nothing any of us have found that is attached to the other realm," Sabrina added.

Gavin lifted and lowered his broad shoulders and Aubrey swallowed to keep from drooling. The man was inhumanly beautiful. "Perhaps the dagger Erin found was the one and only item. I am sure Gunther is pulling at straws in hopes of you finding something that will give him an opening to bring chaos to this realm," he said.

"I felt something," Aubrey blurted and instantly regretted it. Why had she said anything? "At least I thought I did."

"What did you feel?" Erin asked, her curious gaze meeting Aubrey's.

"When I held the dagger. It seemed to get heavier. Just a bit."

Gwen gave a soft smile. "Sometimes when we allow our imagination free rein, it can happen. It was probably nothing more. Like Tristan said. We all touched each item, even spent time alone with them without occurrence."

Padriag looked at Aubrey, his expression tense. "I tried myself. As you are aware, I still have a few magical powers. Other than sensing the passing of time, I didn't get more. We were waiting for you to come home and try."

"Me?" Aubrey wanted to tell them there was no need. A trickle of fear ran down her spine at the idea that if indeed the items were meant for her, she could be in danger.

"Not alone. We will all be with you," Erin assured her.

"Where is Tammie?" Aubrey asked. "Why aren't she and Niall here?"

"She's not feeling well," Gwen replied. "Poor thing has been sick to her stomach all day. Either a stomach bug or she's pregnant."

The men's eyebrows hitched, whilst Erin and Sabrina grinned.

"I hope it's the latter," Aubrey replied.

As she finished her meal, which admittedly was the best food she'd had in a long time, Aubrey took her time drinking a second glass of wine.

"I'm ready," she announced, letting out a long breath.

Was she really?

THE AIR in the cellar was cool since they'd left the window open. Everyone shuffled in, forming a half circle in the crowded the space. The boxes upon which she'd left the wooden box had been moved to the center of a now cleared space. Aubrey walked to it, feeling a pull, as if the items beckoned.

"What should I do?" Aubrey asked, a slight tremble in her voice.

Gwen moved nearer. "Open the box and then take out each item. "Sabrina and I will speak a spell of beckoning."

She wasn't sure what Gwen meant by beckoning, but she didn't bother asking. It was best to get it over with.

Hands over the box, she waited for the chants to begin and then she opened the lid. Inside the items looked to be innocuous. Nothing special, but like Tristan had stated, antique decorations.

First she lifted the bowl and held it. Nothing occurred, no sensations, no bright lights or shivers. Rather disappointing, while at the same time she was glad. When she lifted the pendant, her hand trembled a bit. Mainly because she hoped the creature wouldn't suddenly materialize.

Again, there were no signs.

"I think you're right," Aubrey said, pulling out the dagger. "There is nothing magical about these items." She held the dagger in one hand, and then the other.

There was no change to its weight, no lights, and certainly no glitter.

Aubrey placed the dagger and the pendant on the leather strap into the bowl. "I say we leave all of this be. You all have projects to do, and I have a soon-to-be very successful studio to run. Let's put this all behind us and move on with our lives."

Aubrey smiled at her cousin. "Let's pack up all of this and leave it."

She lifted the bowl and looked at the three items. Something about them gave her pause. Perhaps a part of her had wished for more, to be part of a great adventure like all the others in the room.

"Aubrey," Erin's voice held a tone of hesitance. "Put the bowl down."

"I am putting it into the box. Then I really want to have another glass or two of wine."

Silence.

"Seriously, I mean it when I say we need to leave this and move on. Nothing will happen. I am sure of it."

AUBREY'S VISION BLURRED, everything was going sideways. She'd only had vertigo once, and it had been enough. She'd not noticed any kind of nasal blockage, or her ears feeling clogged like the last time. When she'd had it before, it had lasted about two weeks, and it had been miserable. Nausea and dizzy spells had plagued her making it impossible to do much more than lay in bed and do her best not to throw up.

When the room seemed to right itself, she opened her eyes slowly, bracing for her stomach to protest. Her stomach held steady, and she felt no dizziness, Her vision had cleared everything coming into focus.

"What the..."

She held the bowl with the two items close to her chest and looked around.

The surroundings were completely unfamiliar, and she was alone. She stood in the middle of a long corridor, stone walls on both sides, the floor seemed to be made of packed dirt. Evenly spaced along the walls were iron sconces on which candles' flames provided enough light to see. The slight sway of the flames made for eerie shadows across the floor and up the opposite wall.

This wasn't her house, Aubrey was sure of it. Growing up, she and her father, sometimes with Erin along, had explored every inch of the property. The attic, cellar, and even the shelter that had been dug out of the ground beneath the barn. If something as large as her current surroundings existed, they would have found it.

At the sound of heavy footsteps coming closer, Aubrey ducked into a doorway and flattened herself against the door clutching the bowl closer to her chest. Try as she might to control her breathing, it was hard to do so as an ominous feeling filled her. Something was horribly wrong. She felt it in her bones.

The footfalls continued past her, probably in the corridor that crossed at the end. With a shaky breath, Aubrey peered around the edge of the doorway. At the sight of who walked by, she gasped and ducked back praying with all her might they'd not heard her over the heavy stomps of their feet.

She'd never seen such a being. Muscular, with a thick neck and hairy skin, the creature was huge, well over six feet. They were creatures like those on the pendant she held.

Terror gripped her and a scream threatened. Aubrey pressed her lips together, and covered her mouth with one hand, the entire time gripping the bowl for dear life.

This had to be a nightmare. She'd passed out in the cellar and was now dreaming. That was the only explanation.

If it was a dream, the best thing she could do was to not panic. Yes, she was the heroine of her own action sci-fi movie. First thing heroes did was to find a place to hide that would give them access to communications.

Her legs threatened to fold as she took a few wobbly steps in the direction the creatures had gone. Hopefully, she could slip away in the opposite direction.

Moving slowly, she was glad that she was still in her yoga clothes, which would make it easier to move about. Her joggers were soundless against the flooring as she placed one foot in front of the other.

She'd almost reached the end of the corridor when the sounds of voices came from her right. Whoever spoke did so in a language she didn't understand. Fluent in French, Spanish and Akan, the language of Ghana, which she'd learned from her mother, it was easier to decipher other languages. This one sounded more guttural, and harsh. Russian would sound melodic in comparison.

When one of the voices became louder, harsher, it sent Aubrey's heart into overdrive. The thudding of her heart echoed in her ears, and despite herself, Aubrey was soon sure she'd die there.

Someone grabbed her from behind, one arm around her waist. The opposite hand covered her mouth and dragged her past a doorway and into a room.

"I'm going to let you go, do not make a sound. Do you understand?" a masculine voice with a strong French accent whispered in her ear.

Aubrey couldn't stop shaking as she slowly nodded.

The man released her, and she turned to see a human male. He was tall and slender and wore a tunic and pants that were tucked at the ankles into leather boots. A bit older, she guessed perhaps mid-to-late forties, with silver-streaked brown hair and beard.

He reminded her of an old history professor she'd grown quite fond of in secondary school. That, in itself, made her feel a bit more at ease.

"What are you doing here? Who are you?" He pinned her with a curious expression.

"I have no idea why I'm here," Aubrey replied and then looked around. "One moment I was in my house in Scotland and the next I was here." Tears sprang to her eyes. "Where is this place? What are those creatures?"

The man motioned to a chair. "You are swaying, perhaps it is best if you sit." When she did, he lowered to a chair opposite hers. Between them was what looked to be a small writing table, atop which were several scrolls of paper, a feather quill and a bottle of ink.

"I am called Phillippe, originally from France. I serve as the ruler's scribe." He looked to an arched door. "The throne room is through there, so keep your voice low."

Aubrey looked past him to the door. Those creatures could be in there and she didn't want to be anywhere near them. "I am Aubrey." She swallowed, suspecting the answer, and wishing with all her might that this was a dream. "What is this place?"

For a moment Phillippe studied her. Then he stood and went to a sideboard upon which he moved two glasses closer, lifted a carafe and poured dark liquid into them.

He brought the glasses and placed them on the desk, after sweeping the scrolls aside. "Wine," he clarified. "You will need it for what I must tell you."

It could be poison for all she knew, at the moment, she wasn't sure she cared. When Phillippe lifted his glass, she followed suit drinking at the same time. The wine was delicious, wonderful really. A mixture of dryness with just the right amount of sweetness. It was like no wine she'd ever tasted.

The drink had the desired effect, soothing her nerves just a bit.

"You are in the Dark Realm. It is ruled by Gunther, a human with strong powers."

The Dark Realm. Aubrey felt her eyes widen.

"I must speak to Gunther. He will take me back home. I am sure of it." She started to stand but hesitated when Phillippe lifted a hand.

"At the moment, it is not a good idea." Once again, he glanced at the doorway. "It is not safe. Torants are in there."

Torants. What in the world was a Torant?

"The creatures I saw?" Realizing she still clutched the bowl to her chest, Aubrey lowered it onto her lap and lifted the pendant. "These?"

Phillippe's brow creased as he studied the pendant. "Precisely. How did you come about that item?"

"I found it in the cellar of my house." Aubrey wondered why she was being so open with this man. For all she knew he was evil. After all, he seemed to live here. He'd admitted to being Gunther's scribe. Why had Gunther never told anyone that there was another human in the Dark Realm?

"With those other items?" Phillippe studied the bowl and sheathed dagger.

"Yes," Aubrey admitted, after all, she couldn't very well give another explanation. "Do you know what the pendant is for?"

"I do not," Phillippe replied. "It is curious that you hold a pendant with the depiction of a Torant."

She had to agree. Nothing about what happened made any sense. But then again, since her cousin's involvement with the release of the five knights, nothing had been ordinary. One strange occurrence after the other, so now, this was the latest.

"When can I speak to Gunther?"

Phillippe shook his head. "I do not know. I peered in earlier and, well, there was a disturbance in the air. When darkness falls, it is best to stay away. The appearance of it is deadly to most."

The darkness. Did that mean, Gunther had released it within himself? If that was so, everything could potentially be lost.

She had to get the hell out of here.

CHAPTER FIFTEEN

The air around Gunther tingled, prickling his skin like thousands of miniscule needles. Not painful per se, but to the point that he wanted to remove his clothing and scratch until his skin bled.

He shifted on the throne, barely able to concentrate on the generals who spoke, the entire time shooting him wary looks.

Since the day before, they'd been as tame as puppies, but he knew a deep hatred simmered just beneath the surface.

"Indros, ruler of the Yorian Realm, will arrive before night's fall," Joc was stating. "The border guard has informed us that the of the ruler and his mounted warriors have passed into our territory.

Gunther tried to remember what had occurred, if there had been a discussion or preparation for the meeting, but his memories were hazy. He'd come to on the floor behind a piece of furniture, not remembering how he'd come to be there. He remembered very little. His last memory was of punishing the generals for something. Unfortunately, he couldn't recall what.

It was best not to let them know that particular fact.

"Scribe!" he called out. Why wasn't the blasted man there? He was always present when the generals, or anyone for that matter, sought to speak to him.

It took longer than usual, by the time Phillippe finally appeared. "I apologize for the delay. I had to collect the necessary items..." the man stopped talking and shuffled to sit at the table and chair next to the throne.

"Can you tell me what was planned for Indros' next visit?" he asked the man in a low voice. "He arrives shortly."

Phillippe met his gaze for a moment, as if searching for something, then lowered it and began turning the pages of a thick tome.

"Ah yes, here we are. You were to come up with a reply to his suggestion that you join forces against Esland."

"Anything else?"

Phillippe spoke in a whisper. "You do not trust him to keep his end of the bargain."

"True," Gunther replied.

Suddenly he sensed a movement, not there in a room, but nearby. All was not as it was supposed to be. A sort of shift in the air was present.

He scanned the room, noting only the generals and guards. Then he descended from the throne and walked past the wide windows, to the balcony.

Everything looked to be as it should, yet he couldn't shake the feeling there was something different. Something tangible and out of place. Once the visit was done, he'd investigate it fully.

The scribe studied Gunther for a moment. "Sire, do you wish for some food to be brought? You haven't eaten since yesterday."

The generals exchanged indecipherable looks.

Gunther waved them away. "Leave and return just before Indros arrives. I do not require anything else from you."

"Master, are we not to discuss how the visit should go?" Kel asked, his voice sounding almost desperate. "You did say you wished for us to come to an agreement about how the army is to be handled."

Delving into the Torant's mind was useless, the ward remained intact. A sign of being betrayed, which meant he needed them gone so that he could prepare fully for whatever was to come.

"Leave me. Return in an hour. I need time alone to consider things."

The generals turned to the guards as if assessing their strength. It didn't matter what they ordered. Gunther was powerful enough to disintegrate them all with but a slight movement of his fingers.

Finally, they bowed and walked out, followed by four guardsmen.

Gunther looked to his personal guard. "Go away."

The guards' eyes rounded. "Master, it is impossible to protect you..."

"Would you really kill your own to protect me?" Gunther interrupted. "I do not believe so. Now do as I say."

Once alone in the room, Gunther let out a sigh and looked at Phillippe. "What is it you are hiding?"

The scribe's expression didn't change and when he delved into his mind, he saw only pictures of food. A large roast, potatoes and a steaming pot of soup. The man was obviously very hungry, or over the decades had grown adept at guarding his thoughts.

"Sire, I do not hide anything from you. May I ask a question?"

Gunther nodded.

The Scribe inhaled. "Have you allowed the darkness full rein? Is it your counsel now?"

Interesting that the man was not afraid to ask such a question. The prickling sensation grew stronger, and Gunther blew out an annoyed breath. "It is contained, but barely."

"I see," Phillippe frowned and slid a glance to the adjoining door that led to his study. "There is someone here. Someone from the other realm."

"Esland?"

Phillippe shook his head. "No sire. From the other side. From Scotland."

"Who is it?" he asked, although he already knew.

His stomach tightened and fear of what could happen threatened to surface. If it was Aubrey, could he defend her from the darkness, from the Torants and soon from the Yorian visitors?

"It is Aubrey," Phillippe informed him. "She is very scared and not sure how she came to be here."

His chest tightened. "Where is she?"

"In the study."

At that moment the door opened, and four servants walked in with platters that were placed atop a long table. After, they stood lined up waiting to serve.

"We will serve ourselves," Gunther said. "Leave now."

There must have been a menace in his voice because they practically ran out of the room.

He took a deep breath and closed his eyes concentrating on the balance of good and evil inside him. It was evident that the darkness was the stronger of the two, however, he was still able to keep it at bay.

"Bring her in."

When Phillippe turned to walk to the doorway, Gunther rushed after him. "No wait. I will fetch her."

He opened the door to an empty space. Aubrey was in the room, but she hid. "Aubrey, it's me."

From behind heavy drapes her face appeared, wide eyes meeting his. Then she pushed the curtains aside and darted to him, tears streaming down her face.

She collided against him. "I am so scared. Please help me go home. I want to go home."

The poor woman shook so hard that, when he wrapped his arms around her, he couldn't still her and figure out what hard item was crushed into his lower chest.

"I-I was in the c-cellar and...and then I-I was here. I am s-so very sc-scared."

Pressing his lips to her hair, Gunther whispered. "I am going to help you, but please calm down. There is no need to fret."

Aubrey lifted her head and looked up to him, her brown

eyes filled with so much hope. Even with a flushed face and eyelashes clumped with tears, she was breathtaking. In that instant a feeling like he'd never felt surged. He loved her and would protect this woman with his life.

"Are you hungry?" he asked. "There is food in my...er the throne room."

She glanced to the slightly opened door. "Are those things in there?"

Unsure what she'd seen, he looked to the door, then recalled she'd never seen Torants and had probably caught sight of one.

"No. The only person in there is Phillippe, my scribe."

"I am not very hungry but do wish for something to drink." She searched his face. "Is it safe?"

"Yes." He pressed his lips to hers, hoping to convey calm and assurance. Keeping his arm around her, he steered her through the doorway.

Not releasing whatever it was she clung to, Aubrey allowed him to guide her to the throne room. Upon entering, she gasped, her head moving as she took in the high ceiling, the enormous, ostentatious throne and overly ornate furnishing.

Phillippe stood by the table holding two plates piled with food. "I will take my meal in the study." Not waiting for Gunther's reply, he hurried past.

"Return to perform your duties as scribe when the generals come back," Gunther stated and the scribe nodded and disappeared, closing the door behind him.

Gunther led Aubrey to a chair and lowered to sit next to

her. He was ravenous, but the hunger was not as important as making sure Aubrey calmed, her fears alleviated.

Taking the only other plate left, he placed it between them. He added thinly sliced meat, a few of the other offerings and gave her a fork. Then he poured cider for them.

"It will make me feel better if you eat. I cannot eat in front of you without feeling guilty," Gunther gave her a teasing look.

Her brows lowered. "Okay." She speared a small piece of meat and bit it. After chewing it for a scant second, she ate the rest. "This is very good."

Tearing a chunk of bread, Gunther dipped it into the gravy, placed a piece of meat atop it and ate.

They ate in silence and then Gunther met her gaze. "Tell me what happened just before you found yourself here."

"I was in the cellar with the others, Erin, Padriag, Sabrina, Gwen, Gavin and Tristan. They'd found these three items." She moved back and lifted a bowl with two things in it from her lap. One was a pendant, the other looked to be a case of some sort.

"I picked them up and, next thing I knew, I was here."

He concentrated on the items, not sensing anything. "What are they?"

Aubrey placed the bowl on the table. "A leather necklace with a pendant." He held it up for his inspection. "One of those creatures is etched on it." She pointed to the center of the stone. "In here," she said lifting an oblong item, "is a jeweled dagger. And then there's this bowl that matches."

Indeed, the bowl was made of an amber stone and etched with intricate carvings.

"*Take those things. Destroy them.*" The darkness' voice was so loud, for a moment he thought Aubrey had said it. "*Destroy her, she is the one who will bring our demise. The one who brings the end to all that are these realms. Every soul, every being, every creature.*"

A ringing so loud it was painful filled his head and he cupped both hands over his ears.

"Gunther." A faraway voice said his name. "Gunther, are you okay?"

The voice grew louder. "What's wrong?"

It was Aubrey. She cupped his face, worried eyes searching his face.

"I am fine. Considering what to do." When he slid a glance to the bowl, his body jerked, the darkness urging him to take it.

"A hostile visitor arrives;, I need to get you home before he realizes you're here. Take the items with you. Do you understand? Put them somewhere only you know and do not give them to anyone."

"Not even you?" She asked. "What are they used for?"

Gunther shook his head. "I don't know. I sense they are weapons against the darkness."

She hurriedly lifted the bowl. "What if you need them?"

"You will know if you can trust me. Listen to your heart." He met her gaze.

He enveloped her in his arms and willed them to the other realm. Nothing happened. When he tried again, a feeling like that of knives sinking into his flesh made him stop, as he fought the urge to scream at the pain.

Blowing out a breath, he released Aubrey. "I need time to

find the way to do it. I have brought people from the other realm and taken them back. I am not sure why I can't now.

It was best to get her to safety, somewhere she could rest.

He crossed the room to the study and opened the door finding the scribe who was reading through a large tome.

"I am reviewing notes from the Yorian's last visit, Sire."

"Take Miss Aubrey, through the back corridor, to my bedchamber. Instruct that no one is to go in there." The Scribe gave him a questioning look. "I will ward the room, so that if anyone looks in, they will not see her."

The man visible relaxed. "I will do it immediately. Meanwhile, I suggest you read the notes regarding what we discussed after Indros' last visit."

He turned back and found that Aubrey stood right behind him, obviously still nervous. It was hard not to go with her, to hold her until she calmed. Kiss her until she forgot everything but him. Make love to her, imagining it was only them and not the chaotic situation they found themselves in.

"Go with Phillippe. All will be well. If anyone opens the door to my bedchamber, stay calm, they will not see you."

She leaned her head into his chest. "You promise?"

Gunther cupped her face lifting it so that he could look into her eyes. "I promise."

Her beauty took his breath away. When he returned Aubrey to her realm, he would never seek her again. She deserved so much better than him.

Chapter Sixteen

The bedchamber was like something out of a horror movie. How could Gunther sleep there? The bedcoverings were black, the heavy draperies, a jacquard of sorts, were also black. The furnishings, a huge four-poster bed, nightstands and such, a dark mahogany wood. The only thing on the walls were a pair of swords crossed over the fireplace.

Despite a fire burning, the room was chilly. It was then she noticed the doors to the balcony were cracked open.

Out of curiosity, she opened a wardrobe and found Gunther's clothing. Most of it was also black, except for some button-up shirts in lighter shades, a mixture of grey and blue.

The silence was broken by the sounds of grunts and stomping. She hurried to the balcony doors, but hesitated. Gunther had assured that no one would be able to see her, but it was still terrifying to test the fact.

There was a long black cloak thrown over the back of a

chair. Aubrey took the heavy cloak and pulled it over her shoulders, pulling the hood over her head. Then she walked to the doors, opened them and stepped out.

Dark and gloomy were how she'd describe the surroundings. Spindly trees with crooked branches intertwined stretched out for miles, it was hard to see any ground cover because a thick mist floated across it.

Grunts and stomps sounded again, and she went to the right corner of the balcony from where she could get a clear view of the castle's courtyard.

What looked to be hundreds of creatures stood shoulder to shoulder in straight lines, their faces turned up to another balcony.

"The Yorians will not arrive. I have blocked their ruler from coming," a strange voice, or voices said. "I will not be betrayed."

Chills went up her spine at the words, not because she understood what the voices were referring to, but because it was the most horrible thing she'd ever heard.

She didn't dare to look at the figure who stood not too far from her balcony speaking to the gathering of beings below. It was hard enough to look at those gathered without screaming in terror.

"All who are not loyal will die," the voices said. "We are darkness. We are supreme."

Despite the thick cloak, Aubrey was shivering. The coldness of the air was sharp and cutting. Ever so slowly, she finally worked up the courage to look at who spoke. A scream stuck in her throat.

It was Gunther, but not him. He stood with feet apart,

his arms held out over the crowd. Black veins were visible under his skin, traveling from his arms up his neck and to his face. His mouth was twisted into a sneer as the voices spoke.

Behind him, two of Torants were bound by thick black ropes. They struggled against the bindings without success, both grunting loudly in the strange language she'd heard earlier.

"Death to betrayers!" He shouted, holding up a fist.

The creatures below began chanting, both in English and in their language, seeming to enjoy the suffering of the two who were bound.

Gunther turned to the two hapless males and took one by the throat, lifting him up as if he didn't weigh more than a child.

Aubrey's heart threatened to burst out of her chest, her eyes pinned to what was occurring. Gunther held the creature up as the male struggled, no one daring to interfere. The chanting grew louder and fervent, the pounding of the feet seeming to make the ground quake.

Finally, the male stopped struggling, his body limp and lifeless. Gunther let out a booming growl and threw the lifeless body over the balcony. It landed on the ground with a sickening thud; the limbs twisted in odd angles.

The contents of her stomach churned, but she couldn't look away. What was happening? Why was Gunther acting so savagely?

"We are the ruler." The voices erupted from Gunther's throat as he grabbed another Torant, this one seemed paralyzed by fear, wide eyes moving side to side, mouth agape.

Without hesitation, Gunther tossed him over the balcony

to the ground far below. No one could survive the heights, but this one did. He lay in a growing puddle of blood, lifting a hand up as if asking for help, and then the arm fell limp.

The ones on the ground cheered and grunted, celebrating. It was the most sickening, bizarre display she'd ever seen. Even in movies, something like this would be unbelievable.

When Gunther started to turn in her direction, she shrank back stepping back into the room. She had to get out of there. He wasn't Gunther anymore. The darkness had taken over.

The darkness had won.

Tears poured down her face making it impossible to see clearly. Rushing to the side table, she grabbed the three items and placed the necklace around her neck, then she put the bowl into a pocket inside the cloak. Lastly, she unsheathed the dagger and tucked it into the waistband of her leggings.

How to leave the room was a problem since she was sure guards stood outside the door. She paced and then stopped abruptly catching a glimpse of herself in a mirror.

Her hands flew to her face, her skin felt the same, nothing like the reflection. Was it a mirror or a window" A Torant looked directly at her, its hands moving like hers.

Slowly, with trembling hands, she removed the pendant from her neck and her reflection returned to normal. This was the reason for it. A way for her to hide from others and easily move about the castle.

She replaced the pendant and peered at her reflection. The image made her shudder. Although she looked like a Torant, she was much shorter than the ones she'd seen. No matter, somehow she'd find a way to walk out.

First she grabbed two crystal figurines and then went to stand where the open door would block her from view.

Taking a largest crystal figurine, she threw it with all her might to the floor, picked up a second one and did the same as she screamed.

Within seconds, two Torants rushed in, seeing the room empty, they raced to the balcony. Aubrey circled the door, closed it and noting there was a key in the lock, turned it.

Every part of her shook with fear as she walked as fast as she could down the corridor, then down the stairs retracing the same route Phillippe had used to bring her.

She had to find Prince Sterling, the only person she recalled being mentioned as a friend in the realm. Her mind scrambled, trying to remember if there was a certain way to call upon him, but nothing came to mind.

When she got to the bottom of the stairs, she was thoroughly disoriented. Everything looked the same, dark corridors lit only by sconces. The air smelled musty and felt damp.

Spotting a door, she went to it. When her hand went to the latch, she heard grunts and footsteps.

She pushed the handle downward, it didn't budge. Then she tried pulling it up, but it was locked.

The footsteps came closer. By the frantic grunts, she guessed it to be the guards who'd escaped the room she'd locked them in.

She began walking forward, unsure where the hell the corridor would lead. The Torants closed the distance, and she peered over her shoulder. They rushed closer, stopped and grunted at her.

The language was so strange, she couldn't even begin to

pretend to understand. The only thing she thought to do was to shake her head.

One of them grunted another pair of syllables and shoved her hard against the wall. He pointed toward the opposite end of the hallway, seeming to scold her.

It was then she understood they thought her to be a young one who'd stumbled into the wrong place.

The Torant took her gruffly by the arm to the same doorway she'd tried. He pushed down on the handle that squeaked from lack of use. Opening the door, he shoved her through, grunting something before slamming the door shut.

For a long moment, Aubrey stood stock still, doing her best to ascertain which direction to go in.

Looking up to the grey sky, she prayed for this to all be a bad dream and to wake up in her warm bed. It had to be a bad dream, after all she'd had several of them in the last weeks.

There was a gate, and she hurried toward it. Once past it, she found there to be two paths. One went toward the forest, the other, obviously well used, she figured went to the village where the younger Torants lived.

She headed in the direction of the forest, all the while doing her best to summon help mentally, but unsure of how else to do it.

The tree roots sprouting through the underbrush made for slow progress. But she pressed forward. The air was so cold it permeated through the thick cloak, but she couldn't think about it. She had to find the prince.

Time passed slowly, or quickly, she wasn't sure about the

passage of hours since nothing changed. It was something like twilight. Gloomy and dark.

She constantly stumbled because of the mist and moss covering the ground, plus the long cloak that got tangled on low branches.

Aubrey came to a large tree and looked around. Everything looked the same. "Help me," she whispered, tears streaming down her face.

A low menacing growl followed by what sounded like movement echoed, something or someone was near. Aubrey grabbed the cloak, lifting it from the ground and ran as fast as she could.

After only a few feet, she tripped over something hidden by the mist and she tumbled to the ground, landing on all fours.

A pair of boots came into view, and she was hoisted to stand.

"Why are you out here?" It was Gunther.

Of course, how did she think she could get away without the darkness knowing? It was powerful and probably knew everything that happened in the Dark Realm.

When she moved away from him, Gunther held out both hands signaling her to stop. "I will not hurt you, Aubrey."

He grimaced. "I am keeping the darkness away..."

"Why didn't you force it away when it was killing the Torants? Admit it, you have lost control over it. That was the most heartless, cruel thing I have ever witnessed." Aubrey couldn't stop the tears. "I want to go home."

Lowering his arms, Gunther hung his head. "I cannot take you Aubrey, not without bringing the darkness with me.

It is over for me. It is only a matter of time before I will be consumed by it and lost."

"And you're going to accept it? Not fight it?"

"The others refused to help me. I don't blame them; I probably don't deserve their help. What else can I do?"

His Dutch-accented words were full of sorrow tinged with fear. Aubrey could not imagine how he felt.

"I want to help you, but I have no idea how. What can I do Gunther? I have no magic training, no abilities and yes, my friends won't help."

His blue eyes met hers. "There is no one to blame but me. I agreed to Meliot's terms thinking I was doing good. Thinking I was being heroic." He barked out a dejected laugh. "What a fool I was."

"You were being a hero," Aubrey said. "You thought you were helping your warriors to survive. It is Meliot who is to blame."

She thought about the other two items in the cloak, neither seemed to be appropriate for such a formidable opponent. What could she do with a stupid little bowl and a six-inch dagger? She reached up and removed the pendant from around her neck and held it out. "Would this help in any way?"

He took it, studied it and then held it in his hand, concentrating in silence. "The only magic it gives is to transform whoever wears it. You should keep it for protection," he said handing it back. Aubrey stuffed it into one of the cloak's pockets.

"Is there a magic here? Someone who knows spells?" Aubrey asked.

Gunther started to shake his head and then stopped. "The only one I know of is in Esland. I cannot go near there; they have wards against anyone approaching."

"Can I?" Aubrey asked. "What about Sterling? Will he help?"

"He will not interfere in things having to do with the darkness. It violates Esland laws, and it puts his people at risk."

That was understandable. Sterling ruled a huge realm that had survived centuries by being virtually impenetrable.

"Come, you can speak to Sterling at what used to be my home. I will summon him there. We will ask him to help you return."

"What about helping you?"

Gunther shook his head. "I'm afraid it is too late for me."

Meeting her gaze, he held out his hand. "Trust me. Not always, but right now."

Aubrey hesitated, for a beat. She had no other recourse but to trust him. Despite everything, she believed Gunther was there and fighting to keep control over the darkness.

Their hands touched and she wanted to throw herself against him, to seek the shelter and safety of his embrace, but pictures of what he'd just done, even if it wasn't him, were too fresh.

Gunther seemed to understand. He kept his distance. "Close your eyes. Do not open them until I say."

The ground shifted under her feet. Aubrey almost screamed, but she held her breath for some reason and squeezed her eyes tighter.

CHAPTER SEVENTEEN

"You can open your eyes."

Still unsure, Aubrey waited, then peeked through her lashes. It was what looked like the inside of a cottage, or cabin. If she hadn't known she was elsewhere, she'd think she was back in her own realm.

"You used to live here?"

"Yes," Gunther said. "When I first came here, Meliot made me believe I would live here. I did for years, until one day, his guards came for me." He left the rest unsaid, but after seeing what happened at the castle, Aubrey couldn't imagine what is must have been like for Gunther as a human among those creatures.

He turned away and walked to a window. Through the glass he studied the surroundings, barely moving, his body taut.

It was hard to imagine what he saw, if it was the actual scenery or the landscape of his homeland. She'd been to the

Netherlands several times to visit. It was a beautiful country, which was why she'd gone back.

If ever Gunther were to be released, would he return there?

"I've been to the Netherlands, what used to be the Dutch Republic. It is beautiful. The people are lovely," Aubrey said. She was not exactly sure why she said it, but somehow felt he should know.

When he didn't reply, but seemed to be listening, she continued. "Many people ride bicycles there. I have a friend from university living there. Her name is Uma. She and I rode bicycles every day. Oh, and I was lucky enough to be there during the blooming of the tulips. The display of colors is breathtaking. You would love it."

She inhaled sharply at the last sentence. "I'm sorry, that was insensitive."

Gunther turned, his face expressionless. "No, it is good to hear about my homeland. I am glad that you were able to visit."

"Have you been there, I mean since coming here?"

His chest expanded as he took a deep breath. "Yes, a couple of times. But then I was unable to return. Meliot must have blocked it. So, I stopped trying."

Taking a step closer, his eyes lingered on her face, seeming to trace every part of it, as if memorizing her features. Gunther closed the distance and slowly lifted his hand. Aubrey stood still, unsure of what her reaction would be, at the same time needing his touch.

The feel of his fingers on the side of her jawline sent ripples of awareness through her. The image of his naked body surfaced, the way his muscles rippled with each move, the feel of his skin under her palms as she urged him to move faster, to thrust deeper.

She closed her eyes, unsure what to say to him. How could she reassure or give him comfort when there didn't seem to be a solution to his situation?

"Kiss me, Gunther," Aubrey said.

His mouth claimed hers with the ferocity of a starving man finally given a meal. It wasn't just a kiss, it was a desperate plea, a fierce binding of soul to soul. His arms wrapped around her, unrelenting and warm, while she clung to him as if her touch alone could anchor him to her.

Her fingers tangled in his hair, pulling him closer, silently willing him to hold on. *There has to be a way to save him. There has to be.*

A sound rumbled low in his throat, a deep moan that sent heat spiraling through her. She loved that sound. Loved that it came from him, because of her.

Then, just as abruptly, he pulled away.

"Sterling is here," Gunther said, his voice rough with emotion.

The name snapped her back to reality, though her heart still beat a frantic rhythm in her chest. Without thinking, she smoothed her hair, suddenly self-conscious.

Erin's description flashed in her mind. *A cross between an elf from Lord of the Rings and a K-pop star.* Aubrey scoffed at the absurdity of that image...until the door opened.

Her jaw nearly hit the floor. Her eyes widened so far she half-expected them to roll out of her head. The being who entered wasn't just handsome...he was unreal.

Sterling was ethereal, otherworldly. His fair skin had an opalescent glow, like moonlight on fresh snow. Thick silver lashes framed eyes the color of frosted starlight. Waist-length hair, so pale it shimmered like spun platinum, flowed over his shoulders. His cheekbones were sharp, his jawline sculpted to perfection, as if some divine artisan had shaped him from light itself.

He stood just shy of Gunther's height, lithe but strong, elegant rather than imposing. His tunic, dyed in rich shades of lavender, clung to his frame with exquisite tailoring. The fabric looked impossibly soft, like something between silk and a whisper. Calf-high boots and a slim belt completed the look, regal and effortless.

His gaze flicked to her briefly—cool, assessing—but without malice. Then he turned to Gunther.

Without a word, the two males approached each other, solemn and composed. They placed their right hands on each other's left shoulder in a gesture that felt ritualistic, heavy with meaning.

Aubrey stood frozen, her breath caught in her throat. She wasn't sure what shocked her more, the arrival of a being out of a dream...or the realization that somehow, things had just shifted in a way she couldn't explain.

"You seem unwell," Sterling said, his voice a deep, melodic rumble that matched his ethereal presence. His silver eyes, cool and piercing, fixed on Gunther with concern. "What has become of you, my friend?"

Gunther met the Eslander's gaze without flinching. "It's growing stronger. Stronger than I imagined. I can feel it crawling beneath my skin...waiting."

Sterling's brows drew together in a sharp frown. "Then you should not have summoned me. I will not fight you, Gunther. And I will not kill you."

"If it comes to that," Gunther said quietly, "you must."

A heavy silence followed.

Aubrey's breath caught. "Gunther, no." Her voice trembled. "Why would you ask that of him? There has to be another way. We'll find it."

Sterling turned his gaze on her, the silver eyes assessing her like one might examine an unfamiliar relic. Aubrey instinctively stepped back.

"Who are you?" he asked, his tone not unkind, but threaded with suspicion.

"I am..." she started, but Gunther moved subtly in front of her, placing himself between them with quiet protectiveness.

"She is Aubrey," he said, his voice level. "She requires help to return to her realm. I didn't summon her, she came on her own. And there's no one else with the power to take her. Not that I know of."

Sterling tilted his head, intrigued. "I can take her back, if that's what you wish. But you should ask why she's here before sending her away. If she was drawn to you...she may be part of the answer. Perhaps even the key to breaking free."

Gunther's jaw tightened. "There was hope. Before perhaps. But the darkness has surged in the past days, and I've been unable to keep it at bay. I won't risk her being taken by them."

Aubrey stepped around Gunther, determination burning in her chest and held out the bowl and the dagger. "I found these. I don't think it's a coincidence. Why else would I appear here right after discovering them?"

Sterling arched a brow, the slightest glimmer of curiosity sparking in his otherwise unreadable face. He took the bowl from her hands and turned it over in his palm, his fingers tracing the strange carvings.

"Interesting..." he murmured. "There are bowls like these in Esland. Rare. Often hidden."

He glanced up at Gunther, a spark of something deeper behind his eyes. "Perhaps she's more than an accidental guest. Perhaps she's the beginning of your salvation."

Her heart jumped. "What is it used for?"

"A myriad of things. Mixing of herbs and grasses that are used for ailments or for solidifying spiritual strength."

"What of the opposite, spiritual attachments or attacks?"

Again, the prince shrugged. "I am not a magic, but a warrior. I rarely require a healer or any treatments."

"But there are people in your realm who are prolific in using this bowl?" Aubrey replied. "Do you think one of them, a magic, could save Gunther from the darkness?"

Sterling looked saddened when he shook his head, glancing at Gunther. "It is very likely that whoever attempts to help Gunther will probably be killed by that which binds him. The darkness is very powerful and will fight with all its might not to be taken away from its host. I do not believe it is possible.

"Would you do it?" Sterling asked circling Aubrey, the icy eyes not moving away from her. "Go as far as to risk your life for not only your own kind, but a total stranger?"

Aubrey refused to give up. "He is not a stranger. There has to be someone who is willing to help, a strong magic."

"Stop," Gunther said, putting his hand on Aubrey's shoulder. "Right now, what is important is for you to return to your realm."

Your realm. He'd not said, "our realm." Did he not consider himself part of the human realm anymore?

Aubrey's head snapped at the force when Sterling seized her arm and yanked and spun her, shoving her behind him. A metallic ring echoed as he pulled a sword, its gleaming tip pointed straight at Gunther.

"What..." she began, but the words died in her throat.

"The darkness," Sterling said grimly, "it's consuming him."

Gunther didn't look like Gunther anymore. His form wavered, splitting into multiple versions of himself, four, maybe five, each flickering like a broken reflection in shattered glass. The copies slid apart, then snapped back together in a nauseating rhythm.

Around his boots, shadows coiled, a vile, writhing mist that clung to his legs like living serpents. His muscles strained, cords standing out in his neck as he fought to hold something back. His fists clenched and shook, arms rigid as he battled against an invisible tide.

"Move!" Sterling barked pulling her out of the door dragging her behind a nearby tree. "He's losing control."

"I can't," Aubrey whispered, voice trembling as her eyes filled with tears. "I won't leave him. Not now."

Sterling turned to her, his expression hardening into that

of a monarch, ruthless and absolute. His silver eyes, normally so cold and calm, now burned with urgency.

"Gunther is slipping beyond reach. You must accept it."

But she couldn't.

When Gunther stumbled out of the door, the writing mist rose higher, curling up Gunther's waist like a noose tightening. Black veins etched up his throat, threading like spiderwebs beneath his skin. His features twisted, distorted into something monstrous and unfamiliar.

Still, Aubrey couldn't look away. Neither it seemed could Sterling. They stood frozen, transfixed as the man they knew began to unravel before their eyes.

Then his gaze locked with hers.

Dark, tormented eyes full of agony and pleading. He wasn't gone yet. Not completely. He was begging her.

Help me.

Her heart cracked. She wanted to run to him, to tear the darkness from his body with her bare hands. But she was helpless, just a girl with no power, no plan.

A guttural cry tore from Gunther's chest, raw and inhuman. He dropped to his knees, shaking violently, fighting with everything he had left.

"We are supreme," came the screeching chorus of multiple voices, layered and chilling, echoing from his mouth. "You cannot win against us."

The air turned cold. A seductive apparition shimmered within the dark mist, a pull that twisted at something deep inside her. It whispered promises, offered comfort.

Aubrey swayed.

Sterling grabbed her by the shoulders, eyes blazing.

"Look at me!" he demanded, shaking her hard enough to break the trance. "Do you really want to save him?"

Her breath hitched.

She nodded and then whispered, "More than anything."

Aubrey looked over her shoulder at the now prostrate Gunther. Her chest tightened at what had to be done. "I think he prefers it," she choked out the last word, tears now flowing freely. "He'd rather die than be overtaken by evil."

Sterling held out his hand visibly swallowing. Her hand shook as she placed the jeweled dagger on the Prince's palm.

"God forgive me," she whispered turning to look at Gunther who was now fully engulfed in the dark mist.

Gunther's hand stretched toward them, one final, trembling plea for salvation. His muscular frame shook with the effort, the weight of darkness pressing heavy upon him as he forced himself upright. Knees sinking into the earth, he lifted his quaking arms, palms facing them, as if begging for mercy.

Sterling's voice cracked with emotion. "Goodbye, my friend."

He hurled the dagger, the force behind it so great it cut through the air, the jeweled hilt leaving a ghostly trail of light in its wake. Time seemed to slow as the blade found its mark, burying itself deep in the center of Gunther's chest.

Aubrey's breath caught in her throat, her mouth open in a silent scream.

Gunther's eyes widened, stunned more by release than pain. He met Sterling's gaze, then turned to Aubrey, sorrow and gratitude flickering in his gaze. His lips moved, barely, almost imperceptibly into what might've been a final smile. Then, like a felled oak, he collapsed face-first into the dirt.

Aubrey's scream finally tore through, raw and full of anguish. Her legs buckled, her body swaying as if the very ground beneath her had shifted.

And then the true horror began.

From Gunther's corpse, thick plumes of oily smoke erupted, twisting and writhing like serpents loosed from hell. They screeched as they rose, high-pitched wails that clawed at the mind, forcing Aubrey to slap her hands over her ears as pain lanced through her skull.

The shadows writhed, hungry and untethered.

Sterling seized her hand, his voice a hoarse undertone of urgency. "Run. The darkness is unbound, and it needs a new host, and we're the closest."

Together they fled, hearts pounding, feet crashing through underbrush as the shrieking darkness continued.

They seemed to run for a mile before coming to a clearing. It was not far enough to get away from the sounds the darkness was making. Loud screams in voices that ranged from deep to almost childlike. Almost as if a thousand dark souls filled the air.

Suddenly, a strange, piercing caw shattered the silence above, shrill and otherworldly. Aubrey's pulse leapt in her throat.

"Oh no," she gasped, eyes scanning the sky. "It's coming."

Sterling caught her arm, pulling her into the clearing's heart. "It is not the darkness," he said, voice steady despite the tension in his jaw. "It's Amai, my dragon."

The wind shifted, and then she saw it, at first a speck, then a shadow growing rapidly, impossibly fast. The air trembled around them as the creature descended, immense wings slicing through clouds like sails.

Aubrey's breath caught.

The dragon was enormous and terrifyingly beautiful, its body aglow with iridescent scales that shimmered in hues of violet, silver, and rose-gold. Light rippled over it like sunlight on water, but the sheer size of it, bigger than some houses, eyes glowing like twin opals, made her hesitate. This animal could swallow her in one bite or even roast her with a breath.

It landed in a gust of wind and sound, the earth shuddering beneath its massive weight. Trees swayed, and her hair whipped around her face. Claws the length of her legs sank into the dirt with a low, thunderous crunch. Yet, despite its power, the dragon lowered its head gently and released a deep, melodic trill that sounded like an eerie, almost maternal sound that raised goosebumps on her arms.

"It's calling to us," Sterling said, tugging her forward.

Fear curled around her spine like a vine, tightening with every step. And yet...Amai was mesmerizing. Regal. Unfathomable.

The dragon lifted one colossal foot, holding it steady like a staircase of living armor. Sterling climbed it with practiced ease, then reached down to pull her up, his grip firm, grounding.

As they reached the dragon's back, Aubrey stared at the silken rope Sterling handed her, unsure whether to trust the cloth or her instincts.

"Hold on to this," he said, settling behind her, arms and legs encircling her like a shield. His warmth contrasted with the chill that clung to the air.

Then Amai moved.

Aubrey yelped as the dragon took several bounding strides, earth-quaking, heart-stopping, then launched into the sky. Massive wings unfurled, catching the wind with a deafening *whoomph*, and they soared.

The treetops shrank beneath them, the cottage now just a blur on the horizon, swallowed by the swirling black serpents.

Aubrey clung to the rope, her heart pounding so hard it hammered against her breast. She didn't know what lay ahead, but whatever it was, there was no turning back now.

The wind blasted across her face, blowing her tears dry as soon as they spilled. Her body quaked with grief, a sensation she'd not felt since her grandmother's passing.

Gunther was dead and she'd had a hand in killing him. She was responsible for bringing the dagger. The fact that it was what he preferred, dying over being possessed by evil, didn't soften the overwhelming guilt. What had she done? Why had she been the one to bring the damn things to this realm?

It was hard to tell how long they'd flown before Amai began to descend. Aubrey slumped against Sterling, not caring if it was too intimate as exhaustion consumed her.

How long had she been here? It felt like days since she'd slept. Her head pounded, her limbs ached, and it was impossible to keep her eyes open.

"Relax," Sterling said, his words penetrating her foggy mind. It felt as if he lifted her, moving her with a strange lightness.

Chapter Eighteen

The darkness consumed, ate through flesh and bone, the pain so unbearable, screams erupted from Gunther's throat over and over until he was unable to make any sounds.

When he struggled to get to his knees, to look for Aubrey, it felt as if his muscles were being shredded. Every part of his body quaked with the exertion, but he had to beg for help, he needed to be released.

He would never willingly go into an eternity of cruelty, causing death and destruction to the world. The darkness promised that and more, feeding from his fear, his desperation, growing stronger and easily overcoming him.

Finally, he managed to kneel on the ground and began the fight to raise his arms, giving Sterling a wider target. He met his friend's tortured eyes and had to blink back tears at the raw emotion on the prince's face. With monumental effort, Gunther met Aubrey's gaze, holding it as the dagger flew through the air, behind it a beautiful trail of light and promise.

There was no pain as the blade plunged deep into him, piercing past skin, sinew and bone. Instantly there was relief as everything turned to black.

The last thing he heard were the shrieks emanating from the darkness and Gunther knew he'd won.

HE'D ALWAYS ENJOYED the rustling sound leaves made when the wind rifled them. It was like a melody; one he'd never heard in the alter realm. For centuries, he'd not felt the warmth of the sun on his face or heard the melodic sounds of bird's song.

In the distance the sounds of rushing water added to the imaginary world around him as he floated in and out, his body seeming to fade and reform. Unable to open his eyes, Gunther accepted that he was in the in-between, a place where the dead traveled through, memories of the past resurfacing. He was thankful that the earthly sensations were the forefront of his experience.

If only he could see the beauty of the world where he once lived and not just hear it. But he was grateful for whatever the moment gave.

The sensations continued, the sounds and scents of daylight, followed by those of night. The chirps of crickets, the frogs' croaks mixing with the melody of babbling water.

Once again, the sun's warmth caressed his face, and Gunther took a shaky breath, wanting more of it, wishing to see it. A beautiful bird's singing soothed his battered soul as he prayed for forgiveness and was sorrowful for those he'd hurt in his long, long lifetime. His prayers were more fervent, asking for transport to a good and peaceful place.

The silence was shattered by a shrieking sound, something like a repetitive wail.

"Over here!" a voice sounded nearby. It was followed by the sounds of footsteps.

It was time, he supposed. But it felt so strangely real. As if whoever hurried toward him was earthly. Strange, he'd never imagined it that way.

Hard as he tried, his eyes would not open, nor could he move.

Something pressed against the side of his neck.

"He has a pulse." The masculine voice was deep.

The sound of heavy breathing, followed by something cold and wet pressed against the opposite side of his face.

"Please move your dog back," the same voice said.

Moments later something rigid was placed around his head and he was jostled, then the sensation of being lifted came.

REPETITIVE BEEPING SOUNDS BROUGHT Gunther out of a haze...somewhat. At least he could finally open his eyes, but only to slits.

The room he was in was much too bright. It was stark, the walls an ugly light gray. On his left the rhythmic beep, beep, beep continued. He tried to look to see what caused the noise, but he didn't have the energy to turn his head.

He closed his eyes, allowing sleep to come.

The next time he woke, the continuous beeping penetrated first, followed by the sounds of a disembodied voice from somewhere. "Doctor Patel to ICU. Doctor Patel to ICU."

Moments later, voices sounded, and two faces appeared looking down at him. One was an olive-skinned woman, her black hair pulled away from her face.

"Can you hear me?" she asked, peering down at him and holding something against his chest. "Nod if you can hear and understand me."

Gunther tried to speak, but there was something in his throat. He nodded.

"I am Doctor Patel. You are at St. John's Hospital in Livingston. In the Intensive Care Unit." She waited for him to nod.

Although he had very little idea what the woman said, other than being in a hospital, he nodded.

"You were badly beaten, stabbed and dumped in a nearby nature walk area. At the moment, you suffer from a broken right collar bone, bruised ribs, and a stab wound on the left side of your chest. Miraculously, the blade, which remained imbedded only nicked your left ventricle." She stopped speaking and studied the beeping machine.

What did all of it mean? Was he alive? If so, how was it possible?

Her warm gaze returned to him. "We performed emergency surgery to your heart and left lung, you lost a lot of blood, and your vitals plummeted, so we put you in a medically induced coma. I will keep you here in the ICU until I am satisfied that your vitals are stable. Let's see if you can breathe on your own."

How long had he been there?

A young woman who was injecting something into a clear tube, gave him a soft smile. "We don't know your name. Whoever attacked you took your wallet."

She patted Gunther's arm. "Doctor Patel is going to remove your breathing tube now. Do your best to relax."

The procedure was very uncomfortable. Gunther gagged several times and when he coughed, his ribs protested vehemently. He was left panting and hurting despite the nurse's reassurance that she'd given him medication for pain; he winced with each breath.

"Very good," Doctor Patel said, once again pressing across his chest the opposite end of an instrument that she'd placed into her ears. "Just a bit of a rumble, but that's to be expected."

The corners of her pretty brown eyes crinkled when she smiled. She spoke to the nurse. "Give him a bit of water."

A thin cylinder was placed between his lips, and he sucked in cool water. The liquid was like an elixir to his parched throat. "More," he croaked.

When he'd drank the second half cup of water, the doctor shook her head. "That's enough for now."

"Can you tell us your name and what happened?" The doctor asked. "The police are interested in coming to talk to you once you are better able to speak."

"Gun...ther." He coughed and winced. "Janssen." Again he coughed and closed his eyes as pain assaulted him.

"Don't say more," Doctor Patel said, squeezing his lower arm. "You can tell us more once it's easier to speak."

The doctor rattled off what he perceived to be instructions to the nurse, looking to him every so often. "Only a bit of water every fifteen minutes. Try to see if he can drink broth in a pair of hours, no more than a cup."

"I will be back to check on you Mr. Janssen," the nurse said, and then both women walked out, leaving him alone with the infernal beeping.

A strange fog overtook Gunther, and no matter how hard he fought, sleep crept into the edges of his mind. He needed to think, to know where exactly he was and why.

Livingston didn't sound like a familiar place, but the women's accents had resembled the same Scottish lilt as Aubrey's.

He struggled to consider what he'd do next, but sleep overtook him.

"HERE WE ARE," the nurse, who'd introduced herself as Anna said, pushing a button that lifted the upper half of the bed and therefore caused him to sit. Gunther's head bobbed as he struggled to wake.

"You are very sensitive to the medication; I'll have to tell Doctor Patel we must use a smaller dosage. You have been asleep for almost four hours."

"How long have I been here?" Gunther's words slurred as he fought to keep his eyes open.

Anna tapped on a black object she pulled from her

pocket. "Four nights. Yes, that's right, tomorrow will be five days. You were in a coma for three days."

"Where is this place?" he croaked out stifling a cough.

"Livingston is in Scotland. By your accent I can tell you are not from here. German perhaps?"

Gunter shook his head. "Netherlands." In actuality, he was from nowhere. After centuries in the other realm, he felt disconnected from this world.

"Oh goodness. Were you traveling when you were assaulted?" Anna asked in a no-nonsense tone. Obviously, he was not the first person to come there without identification and in a bad way.

The nurse pushed a wheeled metal table across the bed just over his lap. "Broth and a few water crackers. Hopefully your stomach can handle it. If you have any problem, push this button." She motioned to a red button on a rectangular object.

"I may as well turn on the telly so you can catch up on things." She pressed a different button, and a picture appeared in an instrument mounted on the wall. He'd seen these before but had never been anywhere long enough to ascertain what it did.

The nurse left, closing the door behind.

What had occurred? Had the darkness followed him? He searched the room for any signs of mists or shadows but saw nothing of interest.

When he reached for his spoon, his shoulder area protested. Ah yes, he's broken something. So, he used his left hand and lifted a cracker to his mouth and chewed slowly.

Four days in the human realm. *How was it possible?* he

repeated over and over mentally as he watched what looked to be two people advising others about what happened in the world.

Once again, his eyelids grew heavy, and he glared at the tubing that was connected to his left arm.

This wasn't the time to lay around. He had to find out what had happened.

Just then the door opened, and a woman walked in. "Mr. Janssen, I am Detective Sergeant Willerton. I have some questions to ask."

CHAPTER NINETEEN

Aubrey was at BreYea. The studio had been bustling with activity all day, brimming over with the excitement of those attending their first classes. Although it was gratifying to see and to sense the positive ambience, sadness circled her, and she allowed it, doing her best to put on a happy face when it was required.

Aubrey blew her nose and wiped her tears from her cheeks. Looking into the mirror, she carefully removed the last remnants of her mascara away. Taking a deep breath, she steadied herself and walked out of the bathroom, a smile in place. It wouldn't do for the owner of the newest hot spot in the village to be seen with swollen eyes.

It had only been five days since she'd returned from the other realm, and the ache in her chest felt as fresh and raw as if it had happened moments ago.

The first two days had passed in a haze, her body present but her mind still caught between two worlds. Upon reappearing in the garden and being spotted by Erin, her cousin had whisked her to the castle, where she recounted every painful detail to the five knights and their partners, each word like tearing open a wound that hadn't had a chance to heal.

When she spoke of Gunther...when she said the words out loud, that he was gone, her composure shattered, and she was unable to keep from crying.

The men listened without emotion, not showing one bit of empathy.

Her voice had cracked when she lashed out. "You may not care what happened to him, but I do. He was kind. He protected me. Until the end."

Tristan, bless him, had tried. "It is clear Gunther was a valiant man," he'd said gently. "None of us wished that fate upon him."

Someone else, she didn't even look to see who, had murmured, "At least his death was swift." As if that was supposed to bring her peace.

Only Erin had cried with her. Her tears spilling over as she reached out and gripped her hand. "It's not fair," she whispered. "After all those years...he was never truly free."

That struck like a bell in a still room. The truth of it silenced everyone.

And in that hush, Aubrey felt it, that quiet, aching realization in their eyes. Not regret, maybe, but recognition. Of how cruel fate had been to a man who had once dared to love, to fight, and in the end, to sacrifice everything.

. . .

THE LAST BEGINNERS' yoga class ended, and people began passing by the front desk on their way out. Some stopped to make small talk, but most of them continued on with nothing more than a wave.

Matt, the new yoga instructor appeared next, a bag over his shoulder. "Gotta run, my boyfriend is taking me out to dinner." He gave her a kiss on both cheeks and hurried out the door.

Within moments, the studio was empty, the only sounds the serene music and gurgling of the tabletop water feature.

Aubrey jumped when her phone rang.

When she answered, a no-nonsense voice replied. "Is this Aubrey Maguire?"

"Yes, who's calling?"

"This is Detective Sergeant Willerton from Livingston CID. I need to speak to you. Are you available? I am about ten minutes from Linlithgow."

AUBREY PACED the length of the reception area in the yoga studio, racking her brain, trying to figure out why the police needed to speak to her. She'd called Erin to ensure all was well, then her parents. Not wishing to alarm them, she used the excuse of planning a dinner at the estate. Everyone was thankfully unharmed, so the police coming to visit was troubling.

A woman approached the entrance and Aubrey unlocked it, letting her in. Just a bit shorter than her, at first glance one could call DS Willerton to be an average looking woman. But one look at her sharp eyes and everything changed. The woman commanded attention. She wore blue slacks, a button-up white blouse and a light blue zip-up jacket. Aubrey guessed they were about the same age, early thirties. Willerton's brown hair was cut bluntly at jaw level, a cut that flattered her square face.

"Miss Maguire?" She held up her credentials. "Detective Meg Willerton."

"Yes please come in, sit down. Can I get you some water? A cup of tea?" Aubrey motioned to the two chairs on the left side of the studio. The blinds were closed so they would not be easily seen from outside.

"A cup of tea would be great," the detective replied. Her cell phone rang, and whilst Aubrey made the tea, the detective took a call, replying with one word, two at the most.

"Yes."

"I know."

"Will do."

Aubrey placed two cups of tea on a small table between the chairs, then went and fetched creamer from the small refrigerator and a sugar dispenser.

The detective added cream to her tea, nothing else. Aubrey added extra sugar to hers, hoping it would calm her nerves.

"What is this about?" Aubrey asked as the detective took a sip of tea and sighed contently.

"Thank you, I needed it." She straightened and met her gaze. "An injured man was discovered at a nature walk in Livingston Tuesday morning. He was badly beaten and unconscious. He'd also been stabbed."

Aubrey couldn't fathom who it could be. Was it Marcus? She'd not seen her ex all week. "Who is he?"

"He claims to know you. His name is Janssen, Gunther Janssen." The detective pinned her with a pointed look. "When was the last time you spoke to Mr. Janssen?"

The cup rattled on the tabletop when she put it down, her hand shaking. "Gunther? Are you sure? Is he blond with bright blue eyes, about six feet three? Muscular build?"

The detective's brow furrowed. "Yes, that describes him perfectly."

Her stomach threatened to revolt. Her heart pounded in her chest so hard; she placed a hand over it. "How is he? Where is he? What happened?"

Willerton let out a breath and eyed her tea. "He is recovering at St. John's intensive care. I am trying to ascertain what happened to him. Who is responsible for leaving him for dead?"

"Dead? Oh my god." Aubrey ran both hands down her cheeks. "I need to go see him."

"Can you answer my questions? Perhaps drink more tea," the detective suggested. "You need to calm down. When was the last time you saw Mr. Janssen?"

Aubrey could barely breathe. There were too many questions whirling in her head. She acquiesced and took a long draw of her tea.

"I saw him last on Monday." He was dead...she left unsaid.

"Where was this? How did he seem to you?"

What could she say? "He stopped by my home. I live at Ashcraig Hall, outside the village."

"And what was his state of mind?"

Aubrey inhaled sharply. She'd been holding her breath. "Fine, I suppose, normal."

"What is the nature of your relationship?" Detective Willerton asked. By the look of expectation, Aubrey surmised Gunther had answered the same question.

What had he said?

"We are friends...er, close friends. We haven't defined our relationship, I would say." Aubrey lowered her eyes. "I really must go see him."

"Do you know of anyone who'd wish him harm?" the detective pressed on.

"No, he isn't from here. It had to be random, robbery?"

Finally, the woman seemed to relent. "He was found without a wallet, no watch. Even his shoes were taken."

Aubrey sipped more of the overly sweet tea, hoping the woman would leave so she could go to the hospital. "Is that all? I really need to go."

"For now, yes." Detective Sergeant Willerton stood, and Aubrey followed suit. "I have your information in case I have more questions or if any of his personal effects are found. Will you bring him to your home then?"

Where else could he go? "Yes, of course."

Following the woman to the door, Aubrey grabbed her purse, ready to lock up. Outside the door, the detective met her gaze.

"I must warn you to be prepared. Mr. Janssen was badly beaten. Although he is recovering, he remains swollen and badly bruised."

Once in her car, Aubrey wasn't sure if she should call someone. Erin was the first person to come to mind, but she wasn't sure her cousin would keep the information to herself.

Secondly, she considered her mother, but this was not the time to tell the entire story of how she'd come to know Gunther. Eventually, she planned to sit with both her parents and tell them about everything that had occurred in the last year and a half. However, now was not the moment.

Finally, she dialed Erin who picked up on the second ring.

"How are you holding up?"

"Still very sad. Now I'm very confused," Aubrey said and then hurriedly explained everything to Erin, who interjected with exclamations of surprise and confusion.

Aubrey took a breath. "I am not sure what happened, but I have to find out. I'm headed to St. John's."

"What if..." Erin began. "The darkness..."

"I have my suspicions as to how he came to be here," Aubrey interrupted. "If what I think is true, then we don't have to worry about any evil being attached to him."

"But how will you know for sure? I insist you wait and not go alone. Padriag should come with you."

She wasn't about to sit around and wait for Padriag. It would mean having to explain the new situation and then field more questions.

"You can tell him if you feel you have to. I am heading there now and, when he's released, I plan to bring him to the house."

The drive should've taken twenty minutes. It felt like

fifty. Every red light was a personal affront, and by the time she reached the hospital, her nerves were coiled tight. The parking lot was a nightmare. She circled again and again, heart pounding louder with every pass. Finally, a set of brake lights blinked ahead. She hit her turn signal and slid into the spot the second the other car cleared it.

Her hands trembled as she pulled the keys from the ignition. *Get it together,* she told herself, but her stomach churned with nerves. What if she couldn't get in to see him? If Gunther was in the Intensive Care Unit, would they even let her in?

Inside, the sterile smell helped steady her, but only a bit. She followed the signs toward Intensive Care, her footsteps too fast, her breathing uneven. At the nurses' station, she didn't hesitate. "I'm Gunther Janssen's fiancée," she said, voice steady, face calm, heart hammering like mad.

The nurse glanced at her screen, then gave a small nod. "He's been moved to a standard room. Fourth floor."

Relief hit so hard it nearly buckled her knees. She muttered a quick thank you and practically ran to the elevator, jabbing the button like her life depended on it. When the doors opened on the fourth floor, she didn't pause to look around or second-guess, she walked straight to the room number she'd been given.

No one stopped her. No questions. Just the quiet, antiseptic hallway stretching ahead.

She reached his door and froze, her hand hovering just inches from the handle, her breath snagging in her throat. For one aching heartbeat, she couldn't move. Couldn't breathe. Was it real? Was Gunther on the other side of the door? What if it wasn't him, but a cruel misunderstanding?

Finally, she pushed the door open and stepped inside.

The air in the room was thick with antiseptic and quiet hums from machines. Her gaze landed on him, Gunther, lying very still beneath crisp white sheets. An EKG beeped steadily at his side, wires curling from his chest. An IV snaked into his left arm. His right was cradled in a sling, propped carefully against the pillows.

The detective had warned her that he was injured, but the reality hit harder than she'd prepared for. His face was swollen, mottled with deep bruises, his bottom lip split and bloodied. A swollen black eye was beginning to fade into shades of angry purple and yellow. She could only imagine what bruises hid beneath the gown, on his ribs, his back, his legs. Her stomach twisted.

She didn't dare wake him.

Quietly, she sank into the chair beside his bed, her heart aching just looking at him. The minutes stretched, blurred, softened. She didn't move, just watched the rise and fall of his chest, grounding herself in the rhythm of it.

About an hour had passed when a nurse entered, her smile gentle and knowing. "You must be Aubrey," she said warmly.

Aubrey nodded, eyes flicking back to Gunther. "Has he been awake at all?"

"Only a bit here and there," the nurse replied, checking the machines with practiced ease. "But that's to be expected. He's on strong pain meds for the bruised ribs, and he had both heart and lung surgery. Your friend was in bad shape when he came in."

Aubrey blinked rapidly, tears threatening again. She turned away and wiped her cheeks before they could fall.

The nurse gave her a moment, then spoke again, softer now. "He's making progress, love. Got out of bed today with help, even managed a short walk to the restroom. He's strong. Healing."

Aubrey nodded, swallowing the lump in her throat.

Strong. Yes, he was. But right now, he looked so fragile.

And still, he was alive. That, for now, was enough.

The nurse touched Gunther on his left shoulder, jostling him gently.

"Mr. Janssen, you have a visitor. Time for tea."

His brow furrowed, eyelids fluttering until finally opening. When he noticed her, Gunther seemed to rouse.

The nurse smiled at him. "I'm going to lift you up to a sitting position so you can eat." The bed began lifting his torso up as he winced and let out soft groan.

"Who is your friend?" the nursed asked a still groggy Gunther.

"Aubrey," he murmured. "She is here?"

"Yes, she is here." The nurse motioned for Aubrey to come closer.

Aubrey touched the side of his face. "You will be better soon. I will stay with you."

When he closed his eyes, the nurse spoke loudly. "No more sleeping. Let's get you to drink some juice." She poured juice into a small plastic cup and handed it to Aubrey.

When she brought what looked to be apple juice to his

lips, he drank it greedily. The nurse refilled the cup. "He is always thirsty. It's the medication. Doctor Patel will be weaning him from it over the next two days."

"I wish to leave," Gunther said his eyes half open. "I do not need to remain here."

Aubrey and the nurse exchanged knowing looks. He was barely able to get out of the bed, much less leave the hospital.

After checking Gunther's vitals, the nurse left, promising that food would be coming soon. They were finally alone.

"I thought you'd died," Aubrey blurted out in a low tone, so as not to be overheard. "What happened?"

Gunther shook his head, then scanned her face as if memorizing every detail. "I do not know. I thought I had died, then I woke up here."

Footsteps sounded, but continued past the door. Aubrey leaned closer. "Do you remember anything that can explain how you came to be here?"

"I remember you and Sterling. I was overtaken by..." He stopped, obviously not wishing to bring up the evil that had inhabited him. "Everything went black. I was in so much pain. It was as if something tried to tear me apart."

Judging by the bruising and swelling, it was not an exaggeration.

He looked about to fall asleep again.

"How do you feel? Other than sleepy?"

"The doctor says I respond strongly to medication. She has had to lower the dose, twice."

"Probably because you are from another time and have lived in a realm without modern medicine." Aubrey scanned the machinery, the rhythmic lines of the EKG reassuring.

"Did you know they had to perform surgery in your chest? Gunther, they had to open your rib cage. I am sure that adds to the pain of your bruised ribs."

Doctor Patel visited after Gunther ate. The pretty Indian woman, who had a serious disposition, introduced herself, asked Gunther how he felt and then reviewed Gunther's vitals and checked his incision.

"Nurse Macdougall says you are still sleeping too much. If your pain is tolerable, I am lowering the dose once again," she informed Gunther.

"I am not in too much pain," Gunther replied, then he coughed and groaned.

Doctor Patel looked at Aubrey. "The rib injuries are probably more painful than the surgery. I have prescribed pain medication that shouldn't make him so sleepy. We will see."

"How much longer will he need to stay here?" Aubrey asked. She needed to get Gunther away before they asked too many questions. The stolen wallet excuse would not hold up much longer. They would want to clearly identify him.

"If all goes as it has been, Mr. Janssen should be cleared to leave in two or three days."

After the doctor left, Aubrey turned her full attention to Gunther.

He looked impossibly out of place in the narrow hospital bed. This man, who had once stood like a fortress, sword in hand, unshakable. Now, surrounded by beeping machines and sterile white sheets, he seemed almost too large for the room. And yet, even battered and bandaged, he hadn't lost his commanding presence. Strength still clung to him, something this new world couldn't strip away.

She leaned in, pressing a gentle kiss to his jawline, careful of the bruises. "I'm so glad you're alive," she whispered, her voice catching. "Every day since I came back, I've felt like I could barely breathe. I kept crying for no reason. But now that I know you're going to recover...you're coming home with me, as soon as they let you go."

Gunther reached for her hand with his uninjured left, his touch warm, but unsteady. "I do not wish to be a burden," he said quietly. "I can find somewhere else to stay."

Aubrey arched both brows. "Oh? And how exactly do you plan to pay for it? I doubt landlords here take payment from another realm."

He gave a faint, humorless chuckle, then wiped at his eyes with the back of his hand, wincing as he moved. "As it happens...I have neither gold nor coin. And I'm fairly certain there is not a single part of me that doesn't ache."

When his arm shifted, she caught sight of the deep bruises and angry red gashes along his forearm.

"You're not a burden, Gunther," she said softly, squeezing his hand. "You're mine to worry about now. So, get used to it."

The sun fell, and the view from the hospital room's window turned from dusk into night. Aubrey had remained at Gunther's bedside, not wishing to leave him alone. But she needed to get rest and return the next day. She'd texted Erin to inform her of Gunther's condition and Erin had responded that she and Padriag would come to the hospital with her in the morning.

Gunther was sleeping soundly when she left the room, constantly looking over her shoulder, almost expecting him to disappear.

On the drive home, Aubrey realized she'd not asked Gunther if he sensed any of the darkness. She'd not felt anything, but then again, she didn't expect it. The only way she'd know for sure was if it manifested.

There were two cars at Ashcraig House when she drove up the circular road and parked. She was much too tired to face another round of questions.

Letting out a long, fortifying breath, Aubrey climbed the steps and entered the house. The aroma of cinnamon and other warm spices greeted her. Someone was baking or making something fragrant. She prayed it was biscuits or sweet bread and not just potpourri.

In the kitchen, Gwen was placing scones onto a plate. "Hi Aubrey. I hope you don't mind, but I thought you would appreciate something yummy after the day you've had."

Gwen seemed to be alone.

"Did you come by yourself?"

Gwen nodded. "Yes, I brought Padriag home so Erin wouldn't have to drive to the castle." She smiled brightly. "Their house is making great progress. You must come and see it."

"Tell me everything," Erin rushed in, Padriag sauntering behind, a cellphone to his ear.

"There isn't much to tell. Gunther is heavily medicated, so all I could catch were snippets of information for the few minutes he was awake."

Erin's eyes widened. "His injuries must be horrible."

"That and the doctor says he is very susceptible to the medicine. Apparently they have to keep lowering the dosage."

Gwen placed a scone on a small plate, slid it to Aubrey and placed a fork next to it. "All of them respond to medication differently than those of us that have lived here in this realm. A simple over-the-counter pain reliever is probably just as strong for them as us being given morphine."

"I am going to push for them to release him sooner than two days. Him, there in the hospital, will soon bring questions we can't answer. They've already claimed it was difficult to find anything about him from the Netherlands."

"What about the darkness?" Gwen asked. "Did you ask him about it?"

"I didn't. But I am certain it is gone. I plan to ask him tomorrow. Are you coming?" She asked Padriag, who'd hung up from his call. It was still strange to see him using modern technology, knowing he was born in the sixteen hundreds.

Padriag nodded. "Yes, I was just speaking to the builder, who expected to speak to me in the morning and told him it would be afternoon before I can be out there."

"You are going to have to learn to drive yourself soon," Erin teased.

Gwen held up a hand. "I forgot to tell you that Tristan has finally purchased a car and hired a driver for them. The driver will primarily be used by Padriag. At least until we can figure out a way to get them identities. The lawyer that we trust with the truth is working on it but says it will take time."

Aubrey spoke next. "I've contacted Matt to cover for me at the studio tomorrow and Monday. He is more than willing. I told him I have a sick relative in the hospital, which isn't much of a stretch."

They ate the still-warm scones and discussed plans for the upcoming days. Aubrey wondered how she'd sleep that night, knowing that Gunther was in the same realm.

Chapter Twenty

A Month Later

Gunther walked out of the large home and held his face up to the sun. No matter how many years passed, he knew he would never take the changing skies in this realm for granted.

It had been a month since Aubrey had brought him to Ashcraig, allowing him to recover without much interference. He'd joined the three who lived there for dinner every evening and had spent hours in a sitting room watching television, mostly what they called news, in order to become acclimated to the new world he was to live in now.

Padriag had insisted he remain on the first level in the guest room, which was separate from the rest of them, who slept on the upper floor. Gunther understood. The women had to be protected until everyone was sure he didn't retain evil.

Despite the Padriag's initial resistance, they had formed a rapport, not quite friends, but no longer enemies either.

Gunther looked across the expanse of land to a winding road upon which cars traversed the bends with ease. He followed one in particular, a bright red one because it reminded him of Aubrey's.

"It is a very different world is it not?" Padriag came to stand next to him. "Did you come to this realm often and keep up with the changes?"

Gunther shook his head. "Most of my time was spent in the other realm, I was held captive for an entire century. Meliot did not trust me to travel until in the last few years."

"So, the changes must be stark for you."

"I am not sure I'll ever learn it all, to ever…" He stopped. He'd meant to say, fit in, but it was an obvious observation.

With a chuckle and shake of his head, Padriag shrugged. "All of us feel that way. However, I am glad we've been gifted with the women we have as partners and the remote location we live in. It gives us time to learn at a slower pace."

Another obvious thing to say would be that Gunther didn't have that luxury. Although he was very much attracted to Aubrey and wished for more, she'd been distant since he'd arrived. Friendly and welcoming but seeming to keep him at arm's length.

"What about you and Aubrey?" Padriag asked, seeming to read his mind. "Are you and she going to clear the air? You seem uneasy around each other."

Gunther nodded. "I plan to speak to her." He turned to Padriag, his stomach tight with shame. "Do you know of somewhere I can live. Until I find a way to earn a living, I can only offer to work in exchange for a place to lay my head."

The man nodded. "I do. You can live at one of the cottages at Dunimarle. Tristan and I have already discussed it. You can work at the stables with Gavin or help with construction. First, I suggest you speak to Aubrey. Figure out what's going on in her pretty head."

As SHE PULLED into the driveway and shifted the car into park, Aubrey sank back against the seat with a weary exhale. The house loomed before her, familiar, cozy...and he was there.

Every day, stepping through that front door stirred a storm of emotions. Gunther lived there, and even when he wasn't in the same room, it felt like his presence filled every corner, his quiet strength, his watchful eyes, the scent of him, a bodywash gifted to him by her, that lingered just enough to make her breath catch.

Of course she wanted him there. She wanted him to have a safe space to heal, a roof over his head, warm meals, and someone who cared. But the closeness, the domesticity— they brought more questions than comfort. Gunther's bruises had faded, and lately he'd been testing his range of motion without the sling. Physically, he was healing. But what about the rest?

More than anything, she needed clarity about their relationship. Considering the way she caught him looking at her, feelings were still there. She'd kept her distance, because she didn't want him to feel obligated, physically, emotionally, or otherwise, just because he was living under her roof. And while she missed the warmth of his touch, the easy laughter they'd once shared, she'd rather suffer in silence than risk making him feel bad.

The moment she stepped inside the house, she was greeted by Padriag who was lounging in the front room with that all-too-knowing expression he'd perfected.

"Hi," she said cautiously, eyes scanning the space. "Are you alone? I didn't see Erin's car."

He took her tote bag, his brow arching with practiced drama. "He's in the back garden."

Aubrey's stomach fluttered with nerves.

Padriag stepped closer, lowering his voice. "You two need to talk. Erin and I are getting tired of pretending we don't notice the tension. It's like watching a pot boil while the lid shakes."

She opened her mouth to protest—but the words caught. Instead, she sighed, weary and uncertain. "I will talk to him. I just...I need a few minutes to think."

"Nope." Padriag's hands gently clasped her shoulders as he steered her through the sitting room, into the kitchen and toward the back door. "You've had plenty of minutes. It's time."

He opened the door and nudged her toward it with a small, encouraging smile. "Go."

The sun bathed the garden in golden light, and a soft breeze carried the scent of blooming jasmine and fresh-cut grass. Aubrey paused at the back door, momentarily caught up in the sight before her.

Gunther stood with his back to her, shoulders broad and still, his gaze cast toward the horizon as though searching for something just beyond reach. His hair, now past his shoulders, swayed gently in the breeze, catching the sunlight in glints of gold. She hadn't realized how long it had grown. Padriag had shown him how to use a modern shaver, but a trip to the barber had somehow slipped her mind.

"Your hair grows fast," she said, her voice quiet, almost tentative. "Do you like it that long?"

He turned slightly, giving her a glimpse of his chiseled profile before his gaze drifted back toward the horizon. "I prefer it shorter," he replied. "I didn't notice the time, but it seems you're earlier than usual."

She walked toward him, stopping just a breath away, close, but not quite touching. "I came home early today," she explained. "There's a woman training with Matt at the studio. She's working toward becoming a certified instructor. It gives me a bit more freedom in the afternoons."

Something in his posture shifted, a subtle tension in the line of his shoulders.

"Do you want to go for a walk?" she asked softly. "I want to show you something."

They wandered across the property, feet crunching softly against the gravel path, until they reached a small pond tucked beneath a weeping willow. A bench stood beneath its sweeping branches; the back and legs made from artfully twisted wood that gave the illusion of vines frozen mid-climb.

"My grandfather made it," Aubrey said, settling onto the seat. "It's one of my favorite spots. I come here when I need quiet. Sometimes I journal. Sometimes I just lie back and think."

Gunther joined her, his brows furrowed, the handsome face shadowed. Then, without looking at her, he asked, "Why have you been keeping your distance? Does it trouble you that I'm here?"

Her heart lurched.

"Oh God, no." Her voice was breathless. "I love that you're here."

His eyes met hers then, those piercing, beautiful blue eyes that always made her feel like he could see straight through and into her mind. She nearly sighed at the sheer intensity of him, the way he made even silence feel electric.

"Then why?"

She swallowed hard, her throat suddenly dry, every carefully rehearsed word fleeing her brain. She looked away briefly, then back at him. "It's just...hard," she admitted. "Being around you and pretending I'm unaffected."

He said nothing, just watched her with that unreadable expression.

"I'm so attracted to you," she whispered, cheeks flushing. "But I didn't want you to feel like I expected something—or that you owed me. I didn't want you to feel...obligated."

The words hung in the air, vulnerable and trembling. She didn't dare look away.

"Of course I am indebted to you. To the others. You have offered hospitality and all of you have shared your food, clothes. I have nothing to give in return."

The urge to lean against his chest was almost painful. "It

is not expected. Thankfully, we are all fortunate enough to maintain a good lifestyle."

Gunther turned his gaze back toward the horizon, the sun casting a golden edge along his profile. "This isn't gratitude speaking," he said quietly. "It's not because of what you've done for me. From the moment I first saw you, there's been no one else in my mind, in my heart. But I've never felt deserving of someone like you; someone who cares. My past is flooded with mistakes...sins I can never undo."

Aubrey laid a gentle hand on his arm, feeling the tension there. "You have to let it go," she said softly. "You can't live forever dragging your past behind you like a ball and chain. The way to make peace with it is to move forward, to do good now. To prove to yourself that you're the man I already see."

A soft breeze swept through the garden, sending strands of his long hair across his face. He brushed them aside with his left hand, eyes searching hers. "When you look at me...do you truly see a good man?"

She held his gaze steady, her heart broken at the uncertainly in his. "I do. I see a man who's fought for others, who's survived things most couldn't. A man who's still here, still trying. That takes more strength than most realize."

His eyes fluttered closed, and he leaned forward until his forehead rested against hers. "Thank you," he whispered.

Her heart cracked open at the vulnerable sound of his voice. She lifted her hand to his cheek and pressed a kiss to the edge of his jaw, soft and lingering.

"Can we be friends?" she asked, though even as the

words left her lips, they tasted wrong, too small for what she felt.

Gunther's hands came up to cradle her face, his eyes fierce and tender all at once. "I want to be more than that," he said simply.

Then, with a quiet intensity that stole her breath, he asked, "May I kiss you?"

Aubrey could only nod, her voice lost to the moment. Relief and longing washed through her as he leaned in, his lips firm and seeking, claiming hers in a kiss that said everything they hadn't dared to speak aloud. His tongue slid against hers, slow and sure, and the world seemed to fall away.

When they finally pulled apart, breathless and flushed, Aubrey let out a giddy laugh. "Gunther, I missed you so much."

A slow smile curved his lips. "Not nearly as much as I missed you."

With a joyful sigh, she wrapped her arms around him, burying her face in his chest. He held her tightly, and they sat like that, side by side on the bench beneath the willow, surrounded by birdsong, rustling leaves, and the occasional splash of a fish breaking the pond's surface.

She leaned her head on his shoulder, then noticed his right arm was bare without the sling.

"Does it hurt when I do this?" she asked gently, pulling back to look at him.

He shook his head. "It's well into healing. I just need to be cautious until it's fully mended."

It felt so natural being beside him like this, as if no time or trauma had ever come between them. The peace was almost surreal.

"I need to find a way to support myself," Gunther said, threading his fingers through hers. "I can't keep relying on your kindness."

"You've got options," Aubrey assured him. "Gavin works with horses. Padriag's learning construction. Tristan's a business mogul now, believe it or not. And Liam...well, he still struts around like a lord, but he helps John at the bookshop."

Gunther didn't answer right away. He just sat in thoughtful silence, her hand in his, as if turning over the pieces of a life that might just be beginning.

"What did you do before becoming a warrior for the king?"

Gunther peered up to the sky in thought. "I come from a line of warriors, who followed in the footsteps of their fathers, like I did. One of my brothers was a carpenter, but the rest of us, there were six of us, all fought for King Willem."

"Unfortunately, there isn't a need for a warrior in modern Scotland." Aubrey smiled up at him. "What were your mother and father like?"

His lips curved. "You would think that because my father was a warrior, he was firm. But it was Mother who ruled over our home. She was formidable in a house with seven men. We were fed well, our clothes mended and clean, but she kept a strict house. Chopping wood, clearing the hearth, gardening, caring for the livestock were some of the chores and we gladly did them because she was a worthy woman."

He sighed at the memory. "They have all been gone for a very long time and still, I often remember my family clearly."

"I don't have brothers and sisters. It was just my father, mother and me. My father is from here in Linlithgow, this very house. My mother is from a faraway land where everyone had beautiful skin in many shades of brown. It is called Ghana." She smiled contently. "Both of my parents are kind to a fault. Like with your family, Mum is the one who dealt out punishments when I did wrong. She would send me to my room after supper and, when I got older, I was not allowed to visit friends after school, which was the worst since I didn't have sisters or brothers to spend time with."

He studied her for a moment and smiled. "I can see you being naughty as a child."

"How dare you sir," Aubrey quipped, her lips trembling as she tried to keep a serious face. "Let's figure out what you can do for a living. Tell me what you would like to learn? Name something you find fascinating."

He scratched his jaw in thought. "I am fascinated by the instrument that catches images and freezes a moment."

"It is called photography. Gwen's sister, Sabrina, is a professional photographer, who earns a very good living. I am sure she can teach you."

They continued talking for over an hour, stopping and kissing every so often, each having missed the intimacy of their past.

THAT EVENING, the kitchen was filled with the comforting scent of warm, buttery meat pies. The golden crusts flaked at the touch of a fork, steam rising in fragrant wisps that mingled with the tang of vinaigrette from the fresh garden salad. Erin had set the table with practiced care, candles flickering in mismatched holders that gave the room a soft, welcoming glow.

Laughter had been light, the conversation easy on the surface, at least. But beneath it all, Erin and Padriag exchanged quick glances, subtle nods, and meaningful silences as they stole glances at Aubrey and Gunther. They were trying and failing to mask their curiosity.

Aubrey, for her part, was very aware of it. She could feel Erin's watchful gaze, and Padriag's not-so-subtle attempts to steer the dinner talk toward 'what a beautiful day it had been' and 'how nice a long walk must've felt.'

Gunther sat beside her, calm and composed, but every now and then, his leg brushed hers under the table. Each touch sent a ripple of heat through her, grounding and distracting her all at once.

They lingered over dinner, sipping wine, nibbling the last bites until it was very apparent that Erin and Padriag would not leave things alone until knowing what happened between her and Gunther. Aubrey, cheeks warm from the wine, or perhaps from something deeper, lifted her glass slowly, letting it hover near her lips before she finally spoke.

"I know," she said, voice light but certain, "you two are dying to know what happened between Gunther and me."

Erin set her fork down, eyes wide with innocent amusement, while Padriag arched a brow and leaned in like a man awaiting scandalous gossip.

Aubrey glanced at Gunther, whose eyes met hers with such warmth it sent a shiver down her arms. There was a steadiness in his gaze now, a promise of something stronger than comfort, something real.

She turned back to their waiting friends, her voice quieter but no less sure. "We've decided to explore what this is, what we could be. We're going to take it slow, see where it leads...but we're not ignoring it anymore." She reached for Gunther's hand and laced her fingers with his. "I've asked him to stay. And he's agreed."

For a heartbeat, the room held still.

Then Erin let out a gleeful squeal and raised her wine glass. "To love finding its way!"

Padriag grinned broadly and followed suit, lifting his glass. "About bloody time."

Gunther, ever composed, dipped his head with a small smile, but his fingers tightened gently around Aubrey's. She raised her glass too, heart full, and met the clinks of glass with a quiet joy blooming in her chest.

They sat together a while longer, the meal behind them, yet no one was in a hurry to leave the table. Laughter came easier now. The air felt lighter. And, as the candle flames danced and the night wore on, it felt, for the first time in a long while, that something beautiful was just beginning.

That night, Aubrey lay sprawled across the top of her comforter, the soft cotton of her tank clinging to her skin, her underwear barely offering any warmth. The room was cool, but her body hummed with heat. Her skin tingled, and her cheeks were flushed, not from the wine, but from where her thoughts lingered. Her mind wouldn't settle. Not when the man she wanted was in the room beneath hers.

She rolled onto her side with a frustrated huff, the fabric beneath her rustling as she shifted. Her pulse quickened just imagining him, his strong hands, his steady gaze, the way he'd kissed her earlier with such raw intensity. They'd only just begun to reconnect, to open that long-latched door between them. Would it seem needy if she went to him now? Desperate?

But the longer she lay there, the more ridiculous the idea seemed. She wanted him. Maybe not even for sex, though her body certainly didn't mind the thought, but for closeness, for comfort, for the quiet reassurance of his presence beside her. She didn't want to sleep alone tonight.

Enough second-guessing, she told herself and swung her legs off the bed, her feet padding silently against the cool floor. Her heart beat a little faster with every step down the stairs, her breath shallow, anticipation fluttering in her belly. The hallway was dim, the only light spilling from the moon outside, painting silver across the walls.

When she reached his room, the room that had once been hers, she paused, her hand resting on the doorknob.

She knocked gently, her voice barely above a whisper as she eased the door open. "Gunther? Are you asleep?"

"No," came the groggy, husky reply—his voice thick with sleep and velvet-soft. He had been asleep. Still, he sat up, eyes half-lidded, and extended a hand toward her. "Come here."

Without hesitation, Aubrey crossed the room. She slid beneath the covers, immediately enveloped in the lingering warmth of his body. The bed was cozy, the scent of him, earthy, clean, unmistakably Gunther, settling around her like a second blanket.

"I couldn't sleep," she murmured as she nestled against him.

He wrapped his arms around her from behind, pulling her close, her back flush to his chest. He pressed a gentle kiss to her temple, his lips warm against her skin. "I'm glad you came to me," he whispered, his voice heavy with drowsy affection.

She smiled into the darkness, feeling the steady rhythm of his breathing as it slowed. Within minutes, the soft sound of his snores filled the room, low, even, comforting.

Wrapped in his arms, her body relaxed completely, and for the first time in days, Aubrey drifted into sleep with a full heart and peace in her soul.

A delicious, slow-building sensation stirred Aubrey from sleep. Awareness returned in a hazy wave, and she immediately remembered. Gunther's room. His bed. His arms.

The room was draped in a soft, golden hue, the earliest rays of morning sun spilling through the curtains. The gentle light fell across the sheets and cast just enough light to see.

Her eyes fluttered open, only to fall closed again as a shiver of pleasure swept through her. Gunther's mouth was trailing up the curve of her neck, each press of his lips so tender, so perfect. When he reached the sensitive spot just below her ear, he lingered, his tongue circling slowly, deliberately, until her breath caught in her throat.

She remained facing away, her back tucked snugly against his chest, his warmth surrounding her. His hand, large and sure, slid from her waist, fingertips trailing over her ribs before cupping her breast with reverent care. The contact sent a jolt of sensation through her, and when his tongue flicked gently along the shell of her ear, she couldn't hold back a soft moan.

"Gunther," she whispered, instinctively pressing back into him. Her hips shifted, her bottom brushing against the unmistakable hardness nestled behind her.

He groaned quietly, his breath hot against her skin. The way he touched her, slow, unhurried, full of intent, made her body ache in the most exquisite way.

"Gunther..." she breathed, the word more air than sound, as his fingers teased her nipple through the thin fabric of her top. The friction was delicate yet electrifying, each caress sending trails of heat spiraling to her very core.

Needing him to join her, for his body to react to her touch the way hers did when he caressed her, Aubrey reached between them and encircled his thick erection, slowly moving her hand up and down the silken shaft until rewarded with a husky moan.

The flat of his palm moving down her body, claiming every inch, fueled the flames of passion. Every part of her burned, searing with need. Unable to withstand the wonderful assault as she continued to pleasure him, she threw her head back, turning her face so that he could take her mouth.

Still, both needed, wanted more.

The feel of him, hard and smooth in her hand, was almost too much to take. Silken skin stretched over the taut arousal, seemed to pulse as she stroked him. At the same time, his hands roamed her body, igniting every nerve they passed.

Gunther's breath came hot and uneven, fanning across her neck and shoulder, the sound of it stirring something deep inside her. When his hand slipped beneath the delicate lace of her panties and found her center, her entire body arched in response.

Aubrey barely had time to cry out before his mouth claimed hers, catching the sound and turning it into something deeper, shared, intimate.

"I want you," she gasped against his lips, the words tumbling from her in breathless desperation. "Gunther..."

But she couldn't say more, couldn't think, because his fingers moved with devastating precision, teasing her slowly, coaxing her higher with every soft glide and subtle pressure.

She couldn't resist. Her hips began to move with his rhythm, welcoming the way he slid his fingers deeper inside her, his thumb circling just right, in sync with the rising waves of sensation building low in her belly.

Her hands clutched the sheets as the tension inside her snapped. The climax hit hard, stealing her breath and trembling through every inch of her body. She cried out against his shoulder, her voice muffled by his skin as she shattered in his arms, undone by his touch.

Gunther's heavy breathing fanned her skin as he turned her to lay flat, then climbed over her. His gaze delved into hers. "You are mine."

"I am yours," Aubrey replied, barely able to speak, aching for him all over again. She reached down between them. He groaned when her fingers closed around him.

She guided him to her, running the tip through her slick heat, teasing them both with slow glides. Each stroke sent sparks through her body, and the deep, throaty sounds that escaped him told her he felt it just as intensely.

Her body was on fire, wanting, waiting, desperate, and when he finally entered her, inch by inch, she felt every slow, delicious stretch. He withdrew slightly, then drove back in, deeper this time, his movements steady and purposeful.

She gasped, overwhelmed by the sudden surge of sensation. A second release teased her edges, her body rising eagerly to meet his. She had never felt this way before, like her skin, her blood, her entire being had awakened in his arms.

Her hands slid down his back, fingers tracing the rippling lines of muscle. He was power and grace, every thrust precise, every movement designed to unravel her. His mouth found hers again, kissing, teasing, nipping, each sending sparks to her toes.

Then he lifted her legs and wrapped them around his hips, the angle changing, intensifying. His pace quickened, deep and relentless, and Aubrey could do nothing but surrender to the wildfire building inside her.

She shattered again, crying out his name as the world fell away. He stayed with her through it, still moving within her, until at last he let out a deep, guttural moan.

His body tensed, every muscle taut, before he spilled into her with powerful, pulsing waves that shook him to the core.

For a long moment, neither of them moved. Only the sound of their breathing filled the room, fast and ragged, their bodies slick with heat and sweat.

And just when she thought it was over, when her limbs

felt like silk and her heart couldn't beat any faster, Gunther slid his hand between them once more. His fingers stroked her with a slow, steady rhythm, relentless and tender, until she arched again with a soft cry, fell over the edge one last time.

They collapsed side by side, breathless and entwined, the bedsheets tangled around them. Aubrey blinked up at the ceiling, still catching her breath, her chest rising and falling in sync with his beside her.

She turned her head, meeting his gaze, and in his expression, she saw everything she needed to know.

She was his. And he was very much hers.

"Ohmygod," Aubrey said running the words together. "Your shoulder. I forgot."

He turned to look at her, lips parted as he breathed. "I am not hurt." He sat up and pulled the blankets up to cover them.

Her entire body feeling like jelly, Aubrey snuggled against him and put her head on his chest. "I can't believe it. This was the best sex I've ever had."

His chuckle rumbled under her ear. "I am flattered."

She lifted her head and gave him a playful smirk. "You should be."

Epilogue

"It took you nearly six months to make good on that gathering you promised," her mother, Afryea Maguire, said with a teasing glint in her warm brown eyes. Her voice, laced with its soft African lilt, turned the gentle scolding into music. "But I understand. With your new studio and your handsome new boyfriend, there's been little time left for your boring old parents."

Aubrey bent down and kissed her mother's cheek, the familiar softness of her skin making her smile. "I've already apologized, twice, I think," she said with mock guilt. "Besides, Gunther and I have been by a few times. You and Da haven't been as neglected as you make it sound."

Across the room, Gunther sat with her father, Andrew Maguire, both deep in conversation. Her father was animatedly explaining the finer points of investment strategies, and Gunther listened attentively, his brow furrowed in concentration.

It had taken time, and more than one awkward dinner,

for her parents to fully grasp the truth of Gunther's origins. The first time Erin and Padriag joined them to explain the other realm and the knights' pasts, her parents had exchanged skeptical looks and concerned glances. But after a visit to Dunimarle Castle, and meeting the other knights in person, something had shifted. The evidence was undeniable, and they'd come around.

Since then, her father had taken it upon himself to become Gunther's unofficial mentor. Watching the two of them bond, her dad guiding, Gunther soaking it in with that quiet intensity, was something that filled her heart. It was unexpectedly adorable.

The weather outside was dreary, rain tapping gently against the windows, so they'd all gathered inside Ashcraig House for the gathering. Besides Erin and Padriag, Erin's mother had joined them too, and the lively conversation and clinking of glasses created a cozy warmth inside.

Padriag's story had been easier to tell. Erin's mother already believed in alternate planes of existence. When they shared the truth, she'd clapped her hands and declared she'd be delighted to visit the other realm one day.

That, of course, was never going to happen.

"Gunther, would you help me serve dessert?" Aubrey asked with a sly smile. Then she gave the others a playful warning look. "No peeking. It's a surprise."

She was excited to unveil her cranachan, a traditional Scottish treat she'd made earlier that afternoon. Raspberries, toasted oats, whipped cream with a hint of whiskey, and just the right drizzle of honey. She'd tucked the delicate glasses in the back of the refrigerator to keep them hidden.

"Here." She handed a tray to Gunther. "Hold this, please. I'll just grab the desserts."

But instead of taking the tray, he set it gently on the counter, confusing her.

Then, without a word, he reached for her hands.

Her breath caught as he looked into her eyes with a softness that made her heart flutter. He leaned in and pressed a kiss to her lips, slow and tender, and when he pulled back, there was something nervous, almost boyish, in his expression.

"Aubrey," he said quietly, "I wish to ask you something. I don't know if marriage still exists in this realm...but if it does, will you be my partner for life? Will you be my wife?"

"Oh," she breathed, blinking as if trying to remember how lungs worked. "You...want to marry me?"

"If you wish to," he said gently, the tiniest flicker of uncertainty in his eyes.

Her answer was not so much spoken as felt.

With a happy squeal, Aubrey did a little spin, then launched herself into his arms, looping hers around his neck and burying her face in his shoulder. "Yes! Yes, yes, *yes!* I want nothing more than to spend my life with you. I love you so much."

He kissed her again, right there in the soft, golden light spilling from the open fridge. It was awkward, imperfect, and absolutely perfect.

The cranachan could wait.

This moment was sweeter than anything she could have made.

. . .

IN BED THAT NIGHT, as their breathing slowed, Gunther gathered her into his arms, their bodies still tangled, skin warm and slick from making love. He pressed a kiss to her temple, then whispered against her hair, "You said you loved me."

"I do," Aubrey breathed, her heart fluttering. She thought of teasing him for not saying it back, but she didn't need to. She could feel it in every touch, every look.

"That's good," he said simply. She smiled, loving the way his accent curled around each word.

But then he tilted her face up to his, his gaze piercing, filled with something raw and unguarded. "Because I love you," he said, his voice breaking the silence like a vow. "More than breath. More than life. More than anything I've ever known."

Aubrey's heart clenched, full to the brim. Then he kissed her deeply, as if sealing a promise neither of them would ever break.

Second Epilogue

Gunther was the first to arrive home, the sound of the car pulling away fading into the quiet hum of the afternoon. The familiar sight of Ashcraig House greeted him, solid, unmoving, constant. A strange sensation settled over him as he stepped inside, as if the house itself held its breath.

The moment he crossed the threshold, a sharp meow echoed from the hallway. Oscar, the house cat and reigning monarch of the manor, sat poised with expectant eyes.

"What is it you require, Sir Oscar?" Gunther asked with a faint smile. "Food? A scratch? Or shall I open your private exit?"

Oscar turned, tail straight up, and trotted toward the kitchen, not even glancing back. Gunther followed, expecting the cat to lead him to his food bowl, but instead Oscar went to the back French doors, pawing at one insistently.

"Very well," Gunther muttered with amusement, reaching for the handle. But then he froze.

A familiar figure stood in the garden.

Sterling.

Bathed in a wash of golden sunlight, the prince looked like something he was, a man caught between this world and another. His silver-blond hair caught the breeze, and his otherworldly gaze moved slowly over the garden with curiosity.

Gunther opened the door and stepped out into the warmth of the day. Oscar promptly flopped down on the sunlit step with a satisfied grunt, indifferent to the weight of the moment unfolding.

"You're here," Gunther said softly, approaching Sterling. His voice sounded gruff to his own ears.

"I am," the prince replied, turning his luminous eyes on him. "I had to make sure you were well. I wasn't certain you would...survive."

Gunther stepped closer and placed a hand on Sterling's shoulder, grounding himself in the moment. "It was you who brought me here," he said, though he already knew the answer.

Sterling gave a slight nod.

"I returned to where I'd last seen you...to bury you properly. You deserved the honor of a warrior." His voice caught faintly, just for a second. "Instead, I found you, barely breathing, broken, but alive."

He glanced toward the house, then back at Gunther. "So, I brought you here, to your realm. I thought perhaps your healers could succeed in saving your life. And if not...at least you would be, as you've always wished, in your realm when the end came."

Gunther's throat tightened. The depth of emotion, the unspoken bond, rose like a tide inside him, and he had to blink back tears. "There's no way I can ever repay you for what you've done."

Sterling met his gaze, his expression calm but filled with quiet affection. "It is never about repayment. You are my friend, Gunther. That is enough."

They stood in silence for a moment, the breeze stirring the trees around them, birdsong echoing faintly in the distance. There was nothing else to say. Everything important had already been spoken.

"I won't see you again," Gunther said, his voice husky and he cleared his throat.

Sterling nodded once, the gesture small, solemn. He reached out and placed his hand over Gunther's shoulder, firm, grounding, final, and held his gaze with warmth and something achingly eternal.

Then, he simply faded.

Gunther remained there long after, standing beneath the canopy of leaves, head bowed. Tears slid silently down his cheeks, not of sorrow, but of gratitude.

He was finally home.

And he had been brought there, not by chance, but by a friend who had crossed worlds to give him one last gift.

Also by Hildie McQueen

Erik

Torac

Struan

CLAN ROSS OF THE HEBRIDES

The Lion

The Beast

The Eagle

The Fox

The Stag

The Duke

The Wildcat

The Hunter

The Bear

ROGUES OF THE LOWLANDS

A Rogue to Reform

A Rogue to Forget

A Rogue to Cherish

A Rogue to Ensnare

HISTORICAL SCOTTISH NOVELLAS

Declan's Bride: A Highland Romp

Ian's Bride: A Highland Rom 2

The Lyon's Laird

Medieval Highlander Romance: The Seer

Montana Born & Bred

SHADES OF BLUE

Big Sky Blue

A Different Shade of Blue

The Darkest Blue

Every Blue Moon

Blue Horizon

Montana Blue

Midnight Blue

Shades of Blue Boxed Set

Blue Montana Christmas

HISTORICAL WESTERN ROMANCE

Judith, Bride of Wyoming

Patrick's Proposal

WESTBOUND SERIES

Where the Four Winds Collide

Westbound Awakening

THE FORDS OF NASHVILLE

Even Heroes Cry

The Last Hero

Nobody's Hero

THE MORIAG SERIES

About the Author

USA Today bestselling author Hildie McQueen brings action, romance, and unique settings to life in her captivating stories. From sweeping Scottish historical romance to thrilling contemporary romances, her books offer something for every reader to devour!

When she's not weaving tales, Hildie loves diving into a good book, connecting with fans at events, exploring new places, and spending time with her three adorable pups. She lives in the charming small town in Georgia with her superhero husband, Kurt, who makes every day an adventure.

www.ingramcontent.com/pod-product-compliance
Lightning Source LLC
Chambersburg PA
CBHW020421110726
47899CB00006B/2073